Manny

Manny

Drakken Brotherhood

Book 3

Carol Shaughnessy

GDB After Dark

PUBLISHED BY:
GDB After Dark

Manny
Drakken Brotherhood, Book 3

ISBN 978-1-943095-35-3

Cover by Gina Dyer
Photography by Gina Dyer
Photo credit Depositphoto
Editors Melba Moon, Mary Marvella

Chapter One

Dr. Emerson Laurel watched the burning building fade in his rear-view mirror. He hadn't received a return call from his assistant. She hadn't answered any of his calls, which put him in a mood. He'd gotten out of bed in the raging tropical storm and headed over to find her transformed body stiffened in *rigor mortis*. He didn't hesitate to step over the chilled body. He had things to take care of and not much time to save his lab rats and research. He walked past her the second time after he downloaded the newest research hidden under his personal security code. He set the timer on the reformations he'd had installed as soon as he'd bought the space.

Luckily the building had delivery doors. He dragged each of his test subjects to the SUV and then tossed them inside. The self-destruct countdown gave him twenty minutes to escape with two of his most promising breeders. With the subjects asleep in the back seat, their drugged bodies unable to fight him, he drove the van away from the burning site. He idly wondered why the Brotherhood hadn't taken them. Perhaps they hadn't known how important the women were. Oh well. Soldiers weren't the brightest creatures. They were trained to follow orders. Laurel was happy they excelled at it. Perfect tools. Anger crept into the serenity of his thoughts.

Damn that particular team of interfering misfits. Over time they'd cost him good opportunities. He'd had the perfect partner in Yoseph, gone from him for his protection. He had no idea where the assistant wound up. Yoseph hadn't contacted him. He wasn't supposed to be in touch unless something they hadn't accounted for appeared. Yoseph kept him apprised of the Drakken military team through a close contact.

He couldn't imagine how Yoseph turned one of the loyal guard, but those details made the assistant invaluable.

Looking to the future as he pulled onto the coastal highway, he discovered he missed Jenkins. Discouragement drew a frown. She'd had a cool manner and optimal organization skills, another pawn he'd lost to the insidious Drakken force. He slowed and made a turn. He had to admit Yoseph exceeded her by leaps and bounds, but he'd had to push his former assistant away.

Disgust filled him at the memory of Jenkin's transformation. Her body hadn't formed as he'd wanted. She'd rushed the process. She'd impressed him by wanting to become his female super being. If it had worked he'd certainly be surprised by her successful change. She'd failed by not following his instructions to the letter. The experiment in the desert had borne fruit. Multi-million-dollar fruit, enough that he'd proceeded with the next step in his process. Should he have taken some of her tissue before the current change of plans was executed? What could he have learned from her? A woman in the back murmured in her sleep, breaking that train of thought.

Laurel smiled into the brightening day. He couldn't go far away, yet he wished for the base in the desert. It had been perfect. Now his quarry lived on the east coast, so here he had to stay. Luckily, he'd managed to find a building the CDC no longer inhabited. Always thinking ahead, plan B, plan C, always a backup. It had served him well for years. The habit was well entrenched.

He'd hired new assistants, fraternal twins. The biological research students needed an internship for their doctorates and didn't care about the outcome of the experiments. He'd kept that from Jenkins, convinced the woman who'd fixated on him would spill the beans in a fit of jealousy.

He'd personally processed the paperwork on them because he lacked a trusted assistant. Damn Yoseph for abandoning him. His ire fizzled because Yoseph was still working with him from afar. The day-to-day business was left with wanna-be specialists. But now he'd discovered the perfect replacements. Laurel had found them in the hallowed halls of the technical college in the heart of Atlanta.

He pulled onto the main road, some little two-lane highway

leading away from the coast. He sighed behind the wheel. It wasn't exactly the way he'd imagined this project ending. Still, it seemed he was closing in on the dragons. That thought bolstered his spirits.

In the seat behind him, two breeders carried his next theories to term. He'd soon know if the trajectory he followed was correct or another dead end. The twins would pick up right where Jenkins failed him. Poetic, in a way, he wouldn't have to take care of her when her usefulness faded. He'd noticed her mental state had been sipping.

Sirens wailed, and he dutifully pulled over as the fire truck passed him. His heartrate didn't so much as hiccup. Clear of the emergency vehicles, he pulled back onto the road. The next step in the process already defined by the twins excited him. They were incredibly talented and intelligent, so he couldn't wait to work with them. He put on sunglasses as the road took him north. A black column of smoke split the morning sun. From that fire, like the legendary phoenix, he would rise. Third time is the charm., He'd heard the axiom all his life. This was the third time for him, another pursuit of the fame and secondary wealth he deserved.

***

Rick Carlisle watched Manny Cox walk away. He'd tried to get the stubborn woman to come clean to him but hadn't met with success. She continued to be tighter than a dead clam, and he wasn't sure she'd stick around if he pressed her. Hell, he'd just mentioned talking to her and there she went.

With the mission to rescue Tracy over, he knew the debrief would be later tonight. Keeping his ass in the swing, he'd let her go. Her boots didn't make a sound as she crossed the wooden boards and took the steps, one slow footfall at a time. He watched the swing of her ass, the tail of her braid swept over the curve like a platinum metronome.

The creature, his other half, the Drakken keened softly.

"I know it, bro, but we have to give her time."

Mine.

"I know it, you know it." He got to his feet, hearing Mike and Gareth's vehicle approach. "We have to give her time to figure it out." Rick waited at the porch edge with Manny no longer in sight. Gareth pulled the car up and turned off the engine. Rick tromped down the steps to see the bounty of bags in the back seat. "Do you guys need help?" He glanced at Mike as the tech opened the door on his side. "I thought we were only staying the night."

"It's just a little extra, Mitch texted and said we'd be here a bit longer." Mike told him, stepping back with his arms full. "I don't know about you, but I want to drink a few hours away. I brought my secret recipe makings for sangria." He took his bags inside, his voice fading with distance.

Rick fastened his gaze on Gareth, who shrugged. "Who knows? He's been a little on edge since his kidnapping." Gareth took a gear bag from the back seat.

"I figured you'd put those ghosts to rest, my man." Rick chuckled. He took a share of the grocery bags.

"Not as easy as you'd think." He closed the door behind Rick and followed the retired SEAL into the house. "He's keeping things inside." Gareth spoke softly so no one would overhear.

"That's tough." They exchanged a glance of unity, neither seemed to have mates' forthcoming about their feelings.

Laughter greeted them as Tracy walked past them with BJ on her shoulder, his little face flushed and sleepy. Stepping aside, they let her pass. Moving into the kitchen, they put down the bags and left them for Regina and Mike to unpack.

"Wanna take a walk?" Gareth nodded to the back of the cabin. He kept his voice low with the invitation. With nothing else to occupy him, Rick led the way.

They walked for half a mile. The day held the temperature of winter. The mountains were comfortable, barely in the seventies. With the warm sun and the soft breeze at their back they inhaled the warmth and beauty of spring.

"Something you want to discuss?" Rick broke the silence.

The smell of grilled meat started to drift along their path in the air. Their senses sharpened by the addition of the Drakken DNA, the scent aroused their hunger. The duo had walked nearly a mile, every step quickening as though Gareth wanted to run away.

"I worry about Mike." Gareth halted in his head-long rush.

"Wouldn't have guessed." He tried to keep snark from his voice. Rick shook his head and stopped at a deadfall trunk. He stepped onto the rotting bark and stretched his hamstring. It wasn't that he didn't understand or sympathize. He had his own conflicted feelings for his reluctant mate. His Drakken tensed inside, suddenly hyper aware. Rick glanced around. Was his mate close?

"I'm serious."

"I'm still listening." He turned around and sat down, watching Gareth's boots churning up the ground while he paced. The Drakken kept watch, but didn't actually connect with his female. Rick wondered if Manny headed this way. Where the hell could she have gone?

"He shifted forms the night I took him home. He's so handsome." Gareth couldn't help the gush of love in the words and he didn't try to banish the image of Mike that night. Gareth licked his lips.

His thoughts brought back to the topic at hand, Rick focused. He wasn't sure if Gareth was fighting dryness or buying time. Rick waited, wondering what had the operative on edge. Gareth never experienced nerves of any kind. It brought home the seriousness of whatever weighed on his mind. "That's what we're expecting." Rick tried to encourage Gareth to speak. "All of us need the practice and knowledge. We weren't born this way, so we need to train and develop discipline."

"Yeah, I get it. He was excited but he couldn't catch the wave back to his human form. I helped him, going in and leading him through the process. He hasn't had the same cocky confidence since then." Gareth snorted. "It's like the excitement he discovered in the Drakken was drained away in the flash of panic that hit him. He thought he'd be stuck there."

"I see." Rick didn't actually see the problem. He was there for Gareth, though. Same as he'd be there for any other of the Brotherhood who needed him. He deliberately kept his mind off Manny and his issues with her.

"His Drakken is so new and strong."

"I think you're worrying over nothing. We're all here to train, even Manny, though she hasn't felt the need to shift at all." At least that was the impression she gave. He wondered about that though. Maybe she did feel the need and suppressed it. He should ask Ben about that. The witch knew things. More things than their blood type and how to deliver infants.

***

On a fully leafed oak branch above and to the left of the men,

Manny perched. She'd gone up the trunk after hearing a grunting snort. Figuring it to be a black bear, she gave him or her room to roam. Although spring was pushing through the Smokey Mountains the bear was up early. The last thing she wanted was to tangle with hungry local wildlife.

She watched the round animal lumber away while inside her own chest pressure mounted. She parted her lips, exhaling the resistance away until she was comfortable.

Now she couldn't give away her position. At Rick's approach, another singular feeling imbued her, a curling under her flesh. The touch was soft, for now, a sinuous slide that sparked awareness. She listened to every syllable from his lips, tuned to every nuance of his speech. The words a song her heart danced in rhythm with.

Manny knew the touch of her Drakken. The dynamic beast swirled close to the surface but remained under Manny's flesh. The tanned expanse of her arm darkened and roughened, becoming an attractive pinot noir shade. She closed her eyes and her mouth, biting her lips to keep from making any noise. Her Drakken fought her restriction and Manny worried she'd finally lose control of the beast she hadn't fully accepted. She held her breath until the creature sharing space with her subsided. With a flick of her tail and a last show of scales under her skin the Drakken settled.

This is not over. I will hide as you want, but I disagree.

With that snippet of response a tight feeling coursed her body, as if every pore in her skin, every thought impulse in her mind closed down. Manny returned her focus to her teammates below. She hadn't heard the last of the exchanges. What had she missed?

"You think it's just time we need?" Gareth turned to Rick, hands on hips.

"I think it's what we all need. I also think good ole Murphy and his damn Law has it in for all of us." Rick peeled off bark chunks and tossed them deeper into the trees. "Every time we schedule a takedown based on good intel we miss. We lose our quarry. He gets away." He tore the last piece of bark to splinters. *I wonder if Dolca isn't playing us somehow.* "We aren't going to have much free time until the bastard who poisoned us is captured or killed." That was a priority operation for all of them.

"Where do you think Laurel's gone now?" Gareth dropped his arms and turned toward the cabin. He tipped his head to inhale the faint traces of grilling meat on the air. All the previous tension had left his tone now that he'd had his say and regained his mental equilibrium. The substance of his Drakken pulled back, taking the gray shadow from his skin.

Rick shook his head. *If only all problems were the 'talk it out' variety.* "I think he's staying close to where his last intel told him we were." Rick stood. He inhaled deeply, using his new senses to take in not just the smell of meat but the entire spectrum of scents that filled the air. That little niggle on the edge of his consciousness kept him on edge. Was it Manny? What about this place bothered him? The orange bastard clung to his mental silence.

"You know you ran us out here over a mile?" Rick considered how long the hike back would be.

"Think I can make it back quicker." Gareth grinned at Rick over his shoulder. "Mike started that marinade, basted those steaks." Pride and love swelled his heart, the warmth of the feeling filled his eyes. "That sure smells good."

"You can't shift forms. It's strictly human until dark." Rick warned him, starting the trek back to food. He hadn't seen any sign of Manny. He reasoned she'd likely walked a circle around the cabin and headed back. He wanted to see her, be close. He wanted to know he could reach out and touch her, hold her hand, pull her into a hug or tuck her under his arm. Hell, he might as well wish for the moon.

Instead of gnawing that old bone, he found a pace and rhythm that ate the distance. Every stomp underlined an excuse. He and Manny hadn't had time to come to a comfortable place with public displays. He and Manny hadn't had time to talk about public displays. He and Manny hadn't had time to build near the ease of Gareth and Mike. Damn it, he wanted to get near, but Manny ran the opposite direction. Anger flickered through him and the habit to push it away surfaced.

"We shift tonight?" Gareth jogged to catch up to him. Manny remained immobile in the tree, her gaze focused on their retreating backs.

"I think that's what the commander is planning." Rick's voice faded with distance.

Her heart skipped a beat, the double echo a usual comfort in her chest. When it stuttered realizing Rick moved away from her, irrational fear lit her nerve endings. The sparking pain eased but left her unnerved. Manny scrambled down the trunk, her hands shaking. She stepped onto the forest floor and hugged the tree a bit longer, her knees weak. She turned her head to follow the sound of their voices. Her struggle with her inner creature was much harder than before. The primal reflection of her, the scaled creature birthing within her flesh, needed the one specifically for her.

"He belongs to me." The female's plaintive voice spoke to her, doing her best to force Manny to go to Rick. The woman was strong, so why couldn't she see that strength was exactly what they needed? The Drakkens knew their mates, recognized the need to be together, to spiral in thin air, to make their claims. She disconnected her thoughts and needs from the human. There would be time later to convince the stubborn woman.

"Thank you for hiding me." Manny took a deep breath.

"It is your strength. My purpose to conceal you when asked, when there is need." Her voice sounded sullen in Manny's thoughts. *"I will protect you with this ability."*

Manny released the tree and shook her head. That was unexpected but certainly welcome news. She had an ability that could help her out in combat situations. Since she hadn't been tested like those stationed *Below*, she didn't have mental scores. These discoveries of her mental maturity with the Drakken's influence were surprises.

Straightening as strength filled her, Manny looked after the men. Rick was wrong. She needed to shift, needed to release the power that steadily grew within her. Manny simply resisted changing forms. That was another subject altogether. Once she assumed her form, the animal brain, the dominance of the female dragon would reign. Manny knew enough of her true self to know there would be a fight between her and her mate. He would have to prove his strength to her, his ferocity for her to accept him.

He'd have to fight her tooth and nail, and even then there was no promise he'd best her, overpower her, dominate her and force her submission. She'd never make it easy on him and that fear held her back from joining Rick and her teammates. Manny stumbled. He'd have to defeat her in battle, and she didn't know if Rick could do that and survive. She made her way back to the cabin. It was going to be a long night.

CHAPTER 2

The door stood open on the cabin. The living room light came solely by the flames in the fireplace. All other lights were off. Mitch stood in the wedge of light as he addressed the team. His face in shadow, his soft voice carried into the night. "Tonight all of you who change forms will do so. Under supervision of course." No one uttered a word, but a wave of heady excitement rushed over the assembly. They'd been looking forward to this moment.

In turns strained and yet lighthearted, everyone enjoyed dinner. The food was filling, the company fun and challenging. The family bond strengthened as time passed. The warmth in their hearts lingered even as they filed onto the porch, most wearing robes. Everything was clean, and night had fallen as Mitch addressed the training exercise. Manny stood to one side in deep shadows, invisible to the others. Her arms crossed over her chest. She watched from Mitch's left as he lectured the others.

Gareth held Mike close. She envied them that comfort.

Tracy kept rocking from heels to toes, James beside her, their hands clasped.

Regina stood slightly apart and unmoving, her face in shadow. Manny didn't know where her gaze rested. No doubt it was on her husband. Mitch was a fine-looking man in or out of uniform.

Manny glanced over at Rick, also in shadow. Manny knew his gaze rested on her. The very touch of his attention was a caress she wanted to hold forever. She'd avoided him most of the night, allowing the others to buffer them. When she'd caught a moment alone with Regina, she'd begged her silence.

Regina leaned against the sink edge, hands buried in suds and hot water while they'd talked. "Your blood is Drakken, Manuela."

"No one calls me that, Doctor." Manny stood beside her, back to the sink. She dried a plate and stared blankly across the room. She shivered, the last threshold crossed. She'd admitted her Drakken was awake to one person, Doctor Regina Coombs-Bolton. Manny was capable of shifting forms, capable of mating Rick. For now, fighting the knowledge was all she could do. Manny wanted to puke. She'd had to talk with someone apart from the teams.

"You shouldn't fear any of this." Regina kept her voice just above a whisper. "The majority of us have been Drakken for most of a year. We've learned to control the things we need and love the things we have become." After drying her hands, Regina patted Manny on her rigidly held shoulder. She removed the dish from Manny's tense fingers.

"I'm not afraid. It's a totally different mindset from fear," Manny assured her, but her body remained locked in position. "I don't know if I can explain it." It damn sure wasn't excitement. Maybe it was a form of dread. She watched her hands twist the damp towel. "It means I'm a bigger fighting machine. I'm more danger than demure." Manny searched for the right words, the right statements to help Regina understand. "The last chance the lady has to appear will be lost to a creature from nightmares."

Regina stepped back as Manny pushed off the counter and started pacing.

"It's taking the next step to becoming the *son* instead of the daughter I was born." The tone delivering the statement was uninflected. Yet the toneless delivery didn't hide the bomb she dropped.

Regina led Manny to her home office and closed the door. The history contained in that statement made Regina blink away tears as she moved to her chair and sat down.

"You've been following a path set out for you by your family?" Regina asked after a few breaths.

"JrROTC in senior high, ROTC in college, OCS for another few years, it was my father's dream for his son." Manny checked the doorway, made sure no one was close, turned and paced back. Her hands swung free at her sides, relaxed and open. She'd kept them fisted with stress earlier. Every step reflected her agitation. Manny couldn't hide it as her emotions tumbled free with every confession. "I passed with high marks, worked my enlistments." Manny stopped abruptly and found a place to take a post next to but not in front of the window in Regina's office. Old habits die hard. Her gaze fixed on the window, staring through the glass into the past.

"I guess it wasn't enough?" Regina prompted when Manny fell silent.

"It was everything he dreamed of." She turned to face Regina, her back in the light kept her face in relative shadow. She pressed into the wall, trapped, trying to hide from the words she'd never told another soul. "I was the son he never had, you see. I was the officer that did him proud, but the military is no place for a woman." Manny restarted her track in the room, swinging her arms, pacing silent steps. She lowered her voice, the tone deeper more masculine. "You're not strong enough to stick it out, girls shouldn't play with explosives. You're too smart for the military, why aren't you giving me grandsons?" Manny mimicked a harsher tone.

"Sounds confused."

"He knew every word he spoke. He saw me as a girl but needed me to be his son. I understood it better by the time I refused a second reenlistment. He took off on a bender, landed himself in the hospital with a ruptured ulcer. My mother refused to leave his side and asked me not to visit." Manny stopped again just shy of the rays of the setting sun. She stood with tense shoulders. Regina watched her.

This woman was an integral part of Mitch's mission specialist family. By extension, she belonged to Regina's family by choice. Regina wanted to heal her, make everything better. She sighed in silence. Regina's heart ached for her.

This wasn't something she could slap a bandage on, there was nothing she could excise, no surgery to cut out the cancer that grew in this beautiful and intelligent woman. Regina took a big breath. Except this was all water under the bridge. Manny was living under the yoke installed by her father's unrealistic expectations and her own twist by reaching for them. Listening to the soldier was all she could do. She had the feeling Manuela Vivianna Cox told no one this part of her past.

"I didn't stop by. I didn't write again. Changed my phone

number and dropped out of the family." She turned to face Regina, letting the good doctor see the tracks of tears she'd never shed before. She might not have shed them this evening, except that she'd bypassed the highly touted sangria in favor of bourbon. She followed a simple recipe, fill her glass with the smoky liquor, drink, refill as needed as the sun set. She moved to Regina's side and crouched down. Manny lowered her voice to a whisper.

"If I accept this transformation, it's incredibly strong, masculine." She sniffed but didn't wipe away the tears. "He's won, after all."

Regina slipped to her knees to take the petite woman in a hug.

Manny resisted the motion then gave in to the comfort.

"It isn't what you think. There is strength, but it is feminine. Maybe the most delicate, demure, girly-girl feeling I've ever had." Regina found a chuckle as she released Manny.

Manny smiled without heart. "I'll believe it if it happens." She returned Regina's hug.

"Any time."

***

This night Mitch decided all should change forms. Yet Manny couldn't take that last step. She'd forced Regina to promise not to let Mitch know. The time wasn't now. Manny couldn't reconcile the drive to be strong with the desire to be feminine. Maybe once she and Rick got a little closer the time would right itself. She held back the want working through her, the need of her Drakken to join the rest of the Brotherhood tonight. Torn, she wanted to follow her duty to the others yet the last step of the shift, of taking her form, froze her core until Manny could hardly think. Her Drakken pressed close to the surface and she continually placated the creature to let her human part rule this night. She put on a long sleeved flannel shirt, happy she had now that the Drakken showed her scales. She'd seen them earlier, dark and rich merlot. The creature let them glide under Manny's flesh, a display of her power. Manny kept control with an iron will and no emotion.

Manny wanted to witness the flight of Drakken as they assumed form and took to the skies. Those training and drills she would regret missing. Manny already acknowledged this. The forceful voice of her father already scolded her for not being brave enough to face the trials, the instruction, the courage to let the creature free. Manny admitted she was in a sense letting them all down by her balking. She'd have to work harder to catch up to the rest of the group.

"Into the clearing, the night isn't getting any younger." Mitch's command broke her woolgathering. She straightened but was too slow. Gareth and Mike were running from the house, Rick on their heels.

Mitch took Regina's hand and they followed, moving slower and talking with Tracy and James. A pain in Manny's hand made her look down as blood dripped from the clenched fist. She'd been holding BJ's monitor. There were two bottles in the fridge, and if he woke he'd need one warmed. She was fit only for babysitting duty tonight.

The metal clip cut her hand. She went in to rinse the blood away. Surprised to see the cut heal, she marveled. She was farther along the path to Drakken than she'd realized. That's why the core of her demanded action, pushed her toward a freedom unlike any she could imagine. The creature thirsted for independence, to join with the others. She lashed at Manny's insides, snarling her anger and confusion at Manny's continued restraint.

There was a murmur from the monitor, BJ stirred. Manny hesitated in the doorway.

A pang hit her chest then echoed to a real pain between her eyes. She'd shed her share of tears tonight. There would be no more. A whoosh of air spanked the front of the cabin and she watched a shadow climb into the darkness, clearing the tree tops. Another form followed then two others. Manny looked up. The rest of the team were gone from sight, the clearing at the front of the house deserted. She'd balanced on the balls of her feet when her body strained to join the others. BJ cooed. She glanced down at the monitor she'd clutched too tightly, again. She wiped the drops of blood from unblemished skin.

A soft mental whisper grazed her mind. Her inner Drakken sat up and took notice. Rick came down close to the porch. She found herself caught in his gaze, seeing everything in that moment. He shifted from his Drakken, taking human flesh, human eyes, an all too human expression. Her heart stumbled, scraped along her ribs then righted. He jumped the steps and strode into the cabin.

Manny met him in the great room. One hand held out to stop

his forward movement. "I have to stay." Manny managed to whisper.

"I want you." Rick moved slowly to her, watching every twitch, waiting for her to bolt. She'd done it before. He settled his hands on her arms, realizing again how petite, how fragile. He tightened his hold now he had her. She was always solid, strong, independent enough to make him grind his teeth. This close her features softened, enriched the very feminine soul of Manuela.

"The baby..." She couldn't finish the sentence. His lips claimed hers, took hers, devoured her slowly and with care from the inside. Rick worked his tongue ever deeper, a tangled dance with hers as he learned her flavor.

His body heat scalded her flesh while rousing the Drakken who clamored for release. He held her hard and close but not painfully and Manny began to ease in his hold. She was ready to reach out for him. Her hands braced against his belly, her head tipped back on her neck. A small moan broke from her throat and he swallowed it. Manny dropped the monitor as she clasped Rick close, closer. She lifted one leg, wrapped it around his waist, and pressed until the rasp of clothes began to ignite her anger. She broke free of his kiss, found her arms tightly wrapped around his neck.

BJ, tired of being hungry, filled the room with his howls.

"I have to feed the baby." The airless gasp came out less than a whisper of air.

"Let me go, Pixie. I can wait," Rick told her, his hands supported her ass.

Manny fought conflicting desires. Her brain refused to acknowledge what just happened. Manny fought her way back to sanity. She'd given in to the needs that constantly raked her. The woman and the beast wanted the same thing. The flavor of him lingered on her tongue, her lips. His scent filled the very air she breathed. Manny hadn't realized she'd given so much control to him.

"If the proud parents hear that howl you won't get to babysit anymore." His kissed her, light kisses while the dazed look in her eyes cleared. Rick couldn't get enough of her taste. He wanted time to learn her textures, her responses. He took a deep breath, pulled back.

Manny broke the chokehold around his neck, letting him

lower her body until her feet supported her again. She picked up the monitor and turned it off, walking away from him as if the preceding seconds hadn't happened. The miasma of lust released her, sanity returned.

Rick huffed a deep breath, fighting the wildness that possessed him. He needed to be cool about this. She couldn't leave BJ. He wasn't enjoying the flight without her. His Drakken wanted her claimed as his, but was hesitant and worked Rick's body over with muscle twitches as if trying out moves in a fight. "What the all hells are you preparing for?" he asked the entity sharing his brain space.

"The claiming fight. She will not give in, she is not strong enough."

"You lost me, buddy," Rick told his Drakken, feeling the male stretch against his skin. He closed the front door. His gaze followed Manny as she crossed to get the baby from his room.

"She has had to become too strong to be soft. I know she seems ready, but we must overcome that strength, handle her with gentle force to get her commitment."

"You're going to guide me through all of this, right?" Rick asked in silence as he followed her path down the hall, easily finding them as Manny's voice soothed the grumpy infant. He paused in the doorway, waiting for her as she gathered BJ and took him to the living room. Rick paused at the bathroom, grabbed a robe, and tied the tie as both of his mental halves conferred.

"It will be my pleasure." Content, the Drakken eased back, still hungry for a glimpse of his mate, his female.

CHAPTER 3

In a rocking chair close to the fire, Manny cradled BJ and let the slow momentum calm both her and the baby. "Your mom and dad are flying about. They need extra training. You're stuck with me and a bottle, little man." She couldn't help but smile at the gurgle. He was so fragile, so delicate. Her hands were calloused and her nails nonexistent. They didn't look feminine at all.

"You mean, little Drakken." Rick smiled at her, setting a glass of crystal clear water beside her. The sides frosted since the water came from an artesian well deeply tapped under the mountain's cap.

"Thank you." Manny nodded and turned her gaze back to the infant drinking happily now. She noticed Rick had donned a robe but nothing else. He would be flying more this evening. Her Drakken surged against her very bones, the need to join him, to trumpet her conquest locked her lips for a second.

"You're welcome. And when the others come back, you can have a turn." He leaned back, basking in the fire's glow. They hadn't turned on any other lights and full night at the cabin was stygian in the mountains.

"I don't think I can, Rick. I'm not that far along," she lied to him, again. Manny kept her gaze on BJ, concentration on holding his bottle just right.

"Did Ben tell you that?" Rick suspected she'd been hiding behind the excuse for some time. He hadn't found her out with any evidence, but sometimes his Drakken seemed to know, to sense her closer than Manny let on.

***

Ben had been working on isolating markers to form a timetable. These milestones would tell them how far along the change of DNA from human to shared partnership with the Drakken. The markers Ben isolated and recorded would allow them to follow the course of the infection, for lack of a better term. "If I'm right, the changes in the foundation chain are both guided and random. Your coloring, for instance, is unpredictable. Your advanced healing, on the other hand, is a marker for how far the body is adjusted." Ben briefed them a couple weeks ago.

"All this from a blood sample?" Mike asked from his sprawled position at the conference table.

"Exactly." Ben nodded. "The reason we'd like to keep every drop to ourselves."

"Has there been any progress on finding our vampires?" Mitch asked, attention on the meeting and split to include whatever ranged across his laptop.

"We believe we have the names. Unfortunately, we found them in the obituaries. Both men we photographed were dead within forty-eight hours after collection. Their families had plenty of money to bury them and disappear," Jake chimed in from his satellite feed. The only one of them not expected to become Drakken.

"Laurel." Mitch's tone full of disgust.

"Would be my best guess. He's hired a couple hard-hats for the heavy lifting." Jake scratched under the eye patch that covered the damage to the side of his face. "I am currently trying to find the money trail on all of them, boss man."

"Thank you, Jake. I know you're doing everything you can." Mitch nodded at the monitor. "I guess that's all for now?" He looked at Jake who nodded and leaned forward before the image on the screen went black.

"It's all we have, Mitch."

Mitch looked around the table. "All of you here are now or will eventually become Drakken. Jake has zero exposure. I'm watching for traces to begin taking over in Trevor's blood, but he's not worked with the original six that much to spur it into full blown changes."

"What about you?" Mike asked Ben. He'd been working beside Ben on this, along with Tracy, as needed.

"I believe I haven't been exposed, like Jake. The alteration of my blood will have to combat the rarity of a born witch's power." Ben shrugged. "I'm in contact with the Guardians, you know. They keep me apprised." He looked around the assembly of warriors. His gaze rested a beat longer on Manny.

"Well, in that case..." Mike snorted and straightened in his seat. The others laughed and gathered their notes and got ready to start the day.

"Let me or Mike know if you notice any changes in behavior, nutritional needs, anything that you experience will help us." Ben asked them all, slower to gather his notes.

Down the hallway, Regina and Tracy rushed to fill the table with prepared food, buffet style. They'd snuck out of the meeting moments earlier to assist the caterer, but they'd lingered in the hallway to the end of the meeting.

That was just two days ago, or three?

Manny shook the memories from her mind. She needed to be sharp when dealing with Rick. He was too close to figuring everything out about her. "No, he didn't have the results in last time we spoke."

"I can call him, if you'd like," Rick offered, sipping from his glass. His Drakken studied her through human eyes. Rick let him access the female, patient. The creature would know long before his untrained faculties let the human side know.

"You shouldn't bother him. He takes few enough hours off." Manny put the empty bottle on the table. Standing, she put BJ on her shoulder. She paced the room in front of the fire and cooed back at the infant. She wasn't proud of using the baby as a shield. Manny needed all the help she could gather. She kept her face turned into the baby, hiding her weakness, afraid she'd give away something in her expression. Gently patting the newborn's back, she turned around to make another pass. Her steps slowed as she neared Rick, stopping her forward motion completely when he stood up.

The robe parted and her tongue stuck to the roof of her mouth. They'd gotten close, been in hot situations as a team, worked out in the gym. She'd seen most of his body before and imagined the rest from the skimpy shorts and swim trunks he favored. Rick was taller by a few inches than her five-seven. She guessed he was close to six feet. He easily outweighed her by a most desirable and hunky hundred pounds.

In the firelight the stark white robe reflected the orange flicker framing his length from shoulder to knee with dancing color. Between those reflective columns of light, his flesh glowed with recent exertions. The muscles in his chest moved slowly, calming her, and forcing her to match the ease of his every breath.

Lower, the thinnest line of hair led her captured gaze down as it parted twin halves of a well-defined eight pack. The padding over his hipbones, the ridge led her mesmerized gaze over his hips to stall at the bush curled around the thick base of his cock. The organ stood erect, the crown dark with the blood filling it. The jut of him underlined his need for her.

Manny gulped and turned her back on the most magnificent sight she'd ever seen. She needed a distraction to re-slow her heartbeats, now a double tattoo she'd had to adjust to hearing in her inner ear. To help distract her, BJ burped and filled his diaper at the same time. The noise and smell were unmistakable.

Simultaneously she wished the baby's mother back and that Tracy never return. It insured she'd keep the baby as her shield. Shaking her head, she went down the hallway, eyes perfectly adjusted to the darkness of the cabin, straight to the child's bed to change him.

Rick paced the hallway behind her but kept his silence. He'd stood mute while she ate him with her gaze, visually feasting on his body the way he'd hoped. He wasn't vain, by any means, but he wanted to be sure she got the message. He and his Drakken were tired of her running, blocking, escaping. They wanted her tonight and forever more.

He leaned against the doorjamb to watch as she cooed and whispered while changing the diaper. The sight punched him in the stomach. One day she'd be doing the same with their child. The Drakken fluttered against his skin, a push, a shove that sent Rick out of the room out of the cabin into the night air.

He rubbed his *Solar plexus*, the point of the pain, while he struggled to accept the revelation. The Drakken led him off the porch and took control of the shift. Rick easily found his wings and took to the skies, aiming for the blackness above. Seeking cold comfort in the stars, Rick looked at the future with new eyes.

***

"Where is Rick?" Mitch asked Manny. The team returned to the cabin less than two hours after they'd formed up and left. She stood on the porch, watching as each Drakken landed with grace and skill.

"I thought he went with you." She held BJ while he slept. He'd fallen asleep not long after she changed him. Manny found she was reluctant to give his little body to James. She got to her feet when he went into the house, Tracy right behind.

"He left with us, then split off." Mitch stepped away from the cabin, turning his gaze up to scan the night sky.

"He knows the way home." Regina put her hand on his arm, her gaze solidly fixed on Manny. She knew there was more to the story than a missing operative out on his own.

"He'd better." Mitch stalked into the house. "He should have been at maneuvers."

Regina followed until she reached the steps. Manny's expression was too tight, too controlled. Regina couldn't shake her worry about this reluctant Drakken. "Manny, what happened?" At first Regina didn't think she'd talk. All the relationships between teams had formed, but not into deeper stages of trust and loyalty. She didn't realize how tense she'd become until Manny sighed and dropped her chin to her chest.

"He came back almost immediately." Her voice was barely above a whisper. "He wants the next level, the next step in this relationship. He stood bare before me and I knew." She flapped her hands helplessly. "I didn't know what to do. BJ finished eating and I had to change him and Rick disappeared."

"You ran away." Regina led her back to the swing. "Oh, honey, what were you thinking?"

"I don't know, Regina. Maybe slower. Maybe not sex as obviously as he wanted."

"Are you afraid of physical intimacy?"

The question startled a laugh out of Manny. She was many things, but she'd crossed virginal off the list long ago. "Not at all. I've had sex in relationships. Good sex, even." She shook her head, her eyes searched inward as she stared into the night. "With Rick it feels different." She lifted her hand to her chest. "I have twin beats here now. I didn't tell anyone. The Drakken flexes under my skin, she has opinions and drives. She's strong and sometimes I worry that I'll lose the fight."

"She reflects you, Manuela." Regina held her hand. "She is part of you, but you control the beast." Regina shook her head. "You need to be out there with the others, with me, learning the things you need to control her, to release her power. It isn't a fight, it's more an acceptance of a part of you, you haven't met before. An integration of your strengths."

"She's strong. She will not bend to him." Manny looked at Regina, their gazes locked in the dark. "She'll fight him every step."

Regina had nothing to say about that realization. Maybe she should start investigating the mating practices of the animal kingdom. Not that she'd find dragons, but maybe a key to the male/female dynamic would turn up to help this situation. She hadn't spoken when Manny resumed.

"That's my fear, I guess. That I'll injure him, cripple him and he won't look at me the same as he does now."

"Maybe you should talk this over with him. Get his impression. He's working in a vacuum, you know." Regina squeezed her hand and stood up.

"I'll be here when he comes back." Manny nodded. What Regina told her made sense. Whether she was ready to listen, to put it into practice, was another topic all together.

"Good girl." Regina closed the door behind her, leaving Manny in deep shadows.

CHAPTER 4

"Can we do this with a spinal block?" Laurel demanded. He'd been listening to the whining for hours as he waited on his first birth. The continuous tone worked his last nerve to breaking point.

"Yes, of course, doctor." The midwife bowed and scurried away. She had everything she might need in this facility. Gathering the items, she crossed the hallway and moved up to the bedside.

The nurse took one look at the items in her hands and sighed. "It's early."

"We can't drug her into silence and the doctor isn't a patient man." She handed the things to the nurse. "You'll have to do this. I'll get her up and try to help." She moved to the head of the bed and pulled the woman into a sitting position.

"Up you go, darling. You're doing well. We're going to give you something to help you fill your arms sooner." She pulled the woman's legs to the side of the bed, surprised at the blue flesh. Maybe this was a saving grace for the woman and infant. Yes, the doctor told her beforehand the woman would likely die. She always held out hope.

The nurse readied the needle and gingerly ran her fingers over the protuberant spinal bones until she found the spot she looked for. "This might pinch." The needle slipped easily into place and the woman sighed as relief flooded her body. "Hold on. I need to secure this and we'll get you comfortable."

"Thank you both. I feel so much better already." The woman, still bent over the incredible girth of her waist told the floor.

"That's what we hoped, dear." The midwife eased the woman back as soon as she got the nod.

"It's like tasting heaven after hours of hell."

"I've heard it said." The midwife nodded, folding another sheet over her patient. The woman hadn't noticed her blood puddling on the floor at their feet. The poor child's heart wouldn't beat much longer with nothing left to push through veins and arteries. "You enjoy the rest, when the babe is here, no more rest for you." She smiled into the pale features.

The woman's eyes rolled back, a smile on her face. Under the sheet, her belly heaved as the child moved eager for birth.

"Put her in stirrups and call the doctor. Maybe he'll arrive in time to deliver the infant." The nurse told her, drying her hands. "She isn't going to last much longer."

The midwife did as the nurse instructed.

"About time. I want to see the results." Laurel, already scrubbed and gowned, walked over to the breeder. He peered over the drape at the woman still blissful as death hovered close. "She still with us?"

"Yes, doctor," the nurse assured him. The alerts turned to mute on the machinery hooked to the woman.

"Let's have a baby, shall we?"

***

Rick had nowhere else to go. He had to go back to the cabin. His ride was there, his clothes, his money.

My mate. Stubborn, angered at the delay of their joining, the Drakken barked at him.

She doesn't want us, buddy.

She will be ours, announced in Rick's mind like a royal decree.

Rick was a passenger while the immense orange lizard, second in size to Mitch's great red monster, whined. He reached for patience, his heart battered by the night's circumstances. *What if we're wrong and she isn't the one. What if she isn't changing into a Drakken. Some people must have a natural resistance.*

I know by instinct. She is the only *one.*

Rick banked, recognizing the path he'd walked earlier with Gareth. He was on the cabin quicker than this afternoon. *You talk really well.*

I use your voice, your mannerisms. Distracted but not for long.

Rick pulled his wings, slowing to a drift. Lifting them again, he hovered, then allowed himself to float to the ground. *So there, big guy*. He turned his head to mock an absent Mitch. *Copy that maneuver*. Shifting forms to human, he went to a knee, the pressure a bit much after so long in flight.

"Are you alright?"

The last person he expected outside the cabin rushed to his side. Manny grasped his arm, supporting his weight as he got to his feet. As he steadied she tucked her shoulder under his arm. "Come up and sit down. When you didn't get back with the others, I fixed you a plate."

His nostrils flared at the warm scent of grilled meat. Even the second time around it made his mouth water. "Thank you." He took a seat on the swing, pulling the blanket she'd had wrapped around her over his lap. The inevitable response to being near her rose for her attention. Manny didn't seem to notice. "You didn't have to wait up. I'm a big boy now." He didn't mean it to sound curt. No going back, he sawed off a hunk of warm meat and stuffed it in his mouth. Another mistake that left his mind open for the Drakken's unavoidable comments.

It's a female's duty to wait on you. She should be here for you. You think differently, yet here she is waiting on you, waiting for you. A mental cough. *She waited for us, her mate. She feeds her mate*.

"I was really hungry." Rick sawed off another, smaller, piece of rare delight. He ignored the Drakken under his skin for the moment. He savored the meal and soothed both halves of himself with Manny's closeness.

"I wasn't sleepy and you left rather quickly earlier." Manny leaned against the porch rail, the topper more than wide enough for her to sit on. She crossed booted feet. "It gave me some time to think." She fell silent, wondering what Rick was thinking. He hadn't said much after she gave him the steak.

A chill breeze curled up her spine. She speculated if it were a premonition of things to come. The other Drakken seemed to be experiencing more sensory abilities. Maybe this would be her gift along with her rich wine-colored form. She'd have two abilities, this one and the one that cloaked her. Invisibility still blew her mind.

She'd been thinking of what Mitch said in debrief, along with enough other things to distract her and depress her. Laurel, was still on the run, but now he had babies with their unique genetic structure. Well, pregnant women ,he was continuing with the experiment.

The original six-man team didn't take it well, she recalled. Hating that the mad scientist had slipped through their grasp again. If only there was some way to get ahead of him, figure out what he was thinking. Their only lead Mitch killed. Jenkins helped inseminate those women with modified genetics. Lost in her love for the mad scientist, Amelia Jenkins started her employment in Regina's team of biological researchers. Unable to keep herself from the powerful draw of Emerson Laurel, she'd infected herself on purpose. Manny understood the need now to want to belong.

Jenkins died in the form of a mutant dinosaur, her mental stability questionable. Caution dictated Mitch and Regina study the files on the original six for any sign of instability. There were also the codes on the psychic abilities. So far as Manny knew, there were no tests done with her to reveal any mental add-ins. There were four of in the second team from *Below*. Manny saw their faces as her memory recalled each of them. Jake, their IT spec, Trevor, her younger brother-ish pest, and Benjamin, resident witch and knower of the arcane.

"That was delicious, thank you." The clatter of silver on ceramic brought her out of her thought tangent. "What was it you've been thinking about?" Rick adjusted the blanket. If she was leading him down another dead end he was leaving. It was best before anger pushed him into doing something they'd all regret.

The question tightened her muscles and started the double tattoo of her heart racing. "About us, about what all this means." She waved a hand around the dark porch. She'd told Regina she'd stop running. She had balls enough to see this through. Even Manny got tired of chasing around a subject too long.

"Can you give me a smaller bite of the issue?" He moved over on the swing and patted the cushion. He waited, watched her silhouette as she debated then gave in and slipped silently to his side.

Sometimes the girl was super scary with those movements. Silent as a ghost, she was there and then gone. He pushed a bare foot against the floor, putting the swing in motion. Not sure she'd welcome his arm around her shoulders, he offered her half of the blanket.

Manny pulled the warmth of his body around her. It was natural and she calmed, rather the creature inside her calmed. Manny wasn't sure she'd ever relax again. "Let's just go with us." Manny clutched the folds of fleece in both fists.

"Okay, what's going on with us?" Rick let the night fill the air. If she'd waited up for him, she was ready on some level in her mind. He controlled his impulses to grab her, lift her into his lap. Like he would a deer approaching a hand held out full of corn, he waited on her quietly.

"I like you."

"I like you more, I think."

"I wonder. What if it's the Drakken that chose me, not Richard Carlisle?"

Rick let the silence stretch because he didn't have an answer to that. He pushed the swing, silent on well-oiled grommets, as he thought over her statement. "Okay, I'll give you what I got." He turned to her and put his arm around her shoulders. "I was rescued by you and your team. Thank the goddess and little green men." He watched her smile and another knot inside him eased. "We'd been underground so long I figured we'd die there and I'd made my peace with it.

"I was a lab rat in a study group that went wildly wrong, from some points of view. From others, wildly successful. I have met the Drakken and we are friends. We're closer than anyone can know. You know what I'm talking about?"

"Some of it. The creature is beginning to stir. She knows my moods and echoes my sentiments on the whole." Her stomach knotted at the weak admission. She wondered if Rick would call her on the lies, but he continued as if everything had always been open.

"Right, he's better without a filter, so that's the freshest honest friend I have." He took her hand. "Honey, he's male and he's driven to find a mate. Not every female meets his requirements. You'd have to talk this over with Regina, but genetically there is only one female for him to claim."

"Me." Manny was proud her voice didn't squeak.

"It seems that way. I saw you, hair half-loose, so sexy looking, a smudge of soot or gunpowder on your cheek, and I was in love. My heart kicked hard against my ribs, and I was done for." Rick let that sink in. He never believed in love at first sight. It was important she understood he'd fallen from the moment he'd glimpsed her. "I kept my silence and stood back as we meshed as a team for Mitch. I gave up the service and took a stand to work under the radar for a man I respect and trust." He lifted her hand and kissed her knuckles. "I don't believe in love at first sight, but there was something big that drew me to you."

"I kept waiting for you to notice me, to see me, but I didn't push for your attention. We were barely friends, attracted sure, cause, honey, you're one sexy, smart, beautiful woman." He leaned back in the swing, putting her hand over his heart. "This sounds so slushy, but I think it must have been love at first sight for me. I went out with other women, spent some time with a few. Hey, I'm young and fit." He tried a chuckle, but couldn't pull it off. "You wouldn't leave my thoughts. When Dugan and the team broke the dam in my head, cleaned up the damage and this big orange bastard took over my thoughts? I knew you were the only one." He tapped his temple.

"Rick, trust me. I understand. And someday I'll tell you about what happened with me. Right now, I want to move ahead with you, no rush, no push. Not from you or your Drakken. Not from the purple kid that is living inside me."

"You say the sweetest things, darlin'." This time the chuckle worked for both.

"I have to tell you I'm afraid of this." Manny admitted softly. She stared ahead of them, her gaze fixed on something he couldn't see.

CHAPTER 5

"What do you fear?" Alert, he fixed his gaze on her. The Drakken also woke and studied her. She should not be afraid. Any fear she had he would banish. Their combined gazes roved her face. Rick turned her face to his with a gentle hold on her jaw. She'd been snacking, some of the barbeque sauce dotted her chin. A smear followed the curl of her mouth, making her appear to snarl. He couldn't keep himself from licking his lips and nearly groaned when her gaze dropped to watch the movements.

"I have been alone a long time. I'm not used to having anyone close to me. The closest is my team under Mitch. I'm a tool, a good one, maybe the best in the group. I don't have much female inside or outside." She held up her hand in the darkness, the memory of her earlier study in mind. "That's why Trevor's teasing doesn't make me angry. I can hold my own and every man knows it." She sighed, wishing she had the right words. "I'm not soft, Rick, and if that's what you want, you are going to be disappointed."

"Hey, Manuela, let me worry 'bout that." He took her lips then, moving in so that she didn't have time to pull away. It was one of the best kisses she'd given him and she'd curled his toes a few times. She responded the way he'd wanted, the release of her sexy moan filling his mouth.

Immediately his Drakken surged forward, the animal nature seeking to claim. Rick pushed back and the Drakken settled, not happy but appeased by the closeness of his mate.

Manny pressed close, her Drakken aiding the movement. Power pulsed in her chest, the female inside wanting, needing the closeness of her mate. As soon as Manny comprehended the thought she pulled back, gasping for breath and Rick's lips swept over her cheek, his tongue curled around her ear.

Her hands clenched in his longer than regulation haircut. She liked that he'd let it grow. In the sunlight it faded to strawberry blond, but the curly mass was most often shades of red. She saw his Drakken reflected in his coloring.

"You gonna leave me any hair, darlin'?" Rick whispered against her lips. She gave little puffs of air into his mouth as she fought for breath. He'd licked the honeyed sweetness of the sauce from her lips, cleaned her chin. In the darkness her lids parted, lifted, showing him the nascent glow in her eyes.

While Manny's eyes were a strange mix of amber, khaki and black, her Drakken's eyes was pure wine. How beautiful the color. He smiled at her as her hands released him. The glow of her eyes filled the space between them and she blinked, immediately extinguishing the promising sign. He felt the raised physical evidence of her scales, the blush moved under her tan flesh.

"I'm sorry." She managed to tell him, pulling away.

"I'm not. I want more of your hands on me." He stood up and held out his hand, palm turned up to accept hers. Against his body he could feel the rush of her Drakken growing ever stronger, the pressure like wing beats. "I'd like to continue this inside. Will you join me?"

Manny glanced at the offered hand. Nerves made her knees weak and her hand shake as she slipped it into his larger one. The calluses there gave her a shiver, power in his deceptively relaxed stance. Her work-rough hand filled his palm. He held the blanket to him with his other hand, she wasn't sure if he was shy or protecting her from the sight of him hard and ready.

"I, yes, I would." Manny cleared her throat to get out that much. She let him pull her up. The plate forgotten on the porch, they entered the cabin. Rick led her through the living room with the warm, banked fire. All the other occupants were tucked away and asleep by now.

Inside, the heat made her sweat as they scaled the steps to the loft Rick claimed as his. The door closed behind her and she blinked in the stygian room before the softest light filled the area. A soft whoosh told her Rick dropped the blanket. She stiffened, waiting for the next chapter to begin.

Rick studied her. Back straight, shoulders braced, feet just about shoulder width apart, Manny looked relaxed, but her body coiled to strike. He wanted to touch her, but he didn't want to end up on the floor. "You're not here for inspection, Pixie. You can relax." He spoke softly, walking the five steps to get to her side. He waited while she hesitated. Her shoulders dropped. From there he turned her to face him again. "I thought you might like a little light." He moved his hands slowly to the top button of her shirt. "Feel free to help me." His eyes began to glow. "If you want to stop, don't hesitate to tell me." He slipped the last of the buttons free, parting her shirt to see the delicate lacy cups covering her breasts. Rick clenched his jaw. His next words were forced from between stiff lips. "Oh, darlin', I may not make it through the night."

Manny didn't know if it was his thicker southern accent bleeding through or his irreverent comments, but he made her smile and the curl of arousal slipping through her magnified her pleasure. "Big ole you? Of course, you'll make it."

She pulled the front of the shirt from her waistband, then let it fall open. Her hands moved to the buckle of her belt, only to meet his. She glanced up and stiffened. Hazel eyes gone Drakken glowed green, with the alien pupil a dark line from top to bottom.

"It's still me, Manny." Rick went to his knees, placing a kiss on her stomach, hard as a board. The muscles under his lips tightened as she struggled to find another point of comfort. "Close your eyes, Pixie." He kissed her again, feeling the tremble inside. He didn't stop, pulling the belt free and moving to the button. The zipper was loud on its way down. Manny barely breathed.

"When are you going to attempt a flight?" Rick moved to her boots, his voice strained but easing the intimate moment. He wanted her relaxed, ready but not close to exploding. Right this second she was a short fuse on one of her bombs.

"Wha- Um, flying, yeah." Manny struggled to switch gears, leaving the more perilous road for now. "Soon, I think she's ready." A balm to her scattered emotions.

"Good." He helped her step out of one unlaced boot. "Hands on my shoulders, Pixie." He started on the other, every move sure. He spoke to her as to a child and she responded. "Lift your foot." He put the boots aside. "You have such little feet. They'd be lovely in sandals."

"Can't fight in sandals." Manny said before Rick pulled her jeans over her ass and down her legs.

"I'd protect you." He kissed her abdomen. His heightened sense of smell caught the flood of pheromone rich cream coating her sex. His Drakken flexed and pleasure flooded them both.

Her hands were steady on his shoulders as she worked with him to keep her knees away from his head and still kick off the heavy fabric. Manny shivered as his hands ran up her legs, using enough pressure to prevent any hint of tickling. Higher he worked until his thumbs burrowed under the edges of her boy shorts.

"Rick—" A note close to panic lit her soft cry.

"I got you, don't you worry about a thing."

The roughness in his voice had her looking down. Again the green glow of his Drakken gaze met her stare. "Your Drakken?"

"The lizard is contained. He won't hurt you. He won't interfere." Rick got to his feet, lifting her with his arms crossed under her ass. "Trust me?"

"Yes." Manny knew she could. This first time with Rick was starting to feel like the first time ever. Shivers coursed her body. Chill bumps spread from his touch. The stubble she hadn't noticed before around his jaw abraded her stomach and she enjoyed the roughness. She didn't realize he'd walked to the bed until the coolness of the comforter hit her back.

Rick didn't hesitate, didn't give her the choice of flight. Covering her with his body, he framed her face with his hands, holding her gaze with his. As if reading her mind, he pressed the softest of kisses to her parted lips. "It feels like the first time all over again."

"Me, too." Manny gave him her answer, relaxing under his weight. Not all of it, she knew he kept balance on his elbows and the perfect fit of him between her thighs. "You didn't give me time to undress." Unable to resist, she wriggled her hips and smiled at his pained moan.

"I did not." Rick admitted when he had the breath. "If you keep that up, it won't matter, either." He rolled to his side. His hand sculpted her body from shoulder to hip as he brought her with him. Reaching around her, he cupped her ass. "One thing about a fighting girl, she has the tightest curves." He slipped his hand under the waistband of her shorts, filling his hand with the arc of her ass cheek.

Manny bowed into him. The heat of his palm warmed her flesh and reached deep inside to exposing something wild she'd never known. She pulled away, leaving him with a gasp and going to her knees on the mattress. With a shimmy she tugged the shorts down her thighs, lifting one knee at the time and tossing the jumble of fabric over her head.

"Okay, I'm liking this." Rick propped his head in one hand while the other hand wrapped firmly around his stiff cock.

"Good." She unhooked the bra from the back. With another shimmy her breasts were free.

"You are determined to kill me." He moaned and his grip white knuckled on his cock. Drops of pre-cum rolled like tears down to the crest.

"You have protection?" she asked, moving back to her original spot beside him.

The haze had to clear before his mind reengaged. "Protection, um, yes..." He rolled to the bedside table, pulled a box from the drawer, and tore off the lid. His hands shaking, he watched as Manny calmly chose one, ripped the packet open, and pulled the wrapper free. "I've never had a girl, I mean I usually—" His voice caught as her lips closed over the weeping head of his cock, taking the smear of his excitement with her tongue.

He arched when she hummed at his flavor, His body locked in that position while she gave the flared head a kiss and then rolled the condom into place. He hadn't time to blink before she straddled him, lined their bodies, and took him deep in one plunge. He opened his mouth to yelp, only to find her hand there.

"Shh, the house is sleeping. The fewer who know about this right now, the better." Her pink gaze belied her calm words as she worked herself along his length. Heat and friction bathed his cock and he reached for her hips, helping her ride.

"I'm not going to last."

Manny paused in her ride, the friction between them building to an explosion she both craved and feared. In her line of work combustion of any kind was dangerous. She blinked down at Rick, her hips settled tightly against him. His voice spoke clearly into her head. She knew this with certainty because her hand still cupped his mouth. She wanted to stop, to ask questions, but the creature tied so tightly to Manny wouldn't stop, didn't pause in her rush for orgasm. Urgent demands forced her to ignore the presence of him so intimately connected. The mind link should have scared her, frightened her beyond belief. The Drakken took over.

CHAPTER 6

Manny's body moved out of her control and into autopilot. She ground her pelvis down on Rick, searching for the right pressure point to take her over the edge and into ecstasy. He was long and went deep, deeper than she'd ever experienced with a lover. She was sure she'd be sore tomorrow, but right now nothing was better than the burning stretch of his cock opening her, filling her. She pivoted her hips, finding the right pace, the angle she needed.

Throwing back her head, she remembered the other occupants in the house. In an instant, she curled her body down over Rick's, her mouth open to stifle her scream of orgasm against his chest. As her body tightened then exploded, her mouth itched. Her teeth hurt. She buried her mouth against Rick's pectoral muscle.

Sweet copper blood flooded her mouth. Inside her head an incredible trumpet sounded. Her body out of her control, she swallowed, licked the source. Her mind adrift, Manny's consciousness skated the gray area before crossing the line into darkness.

Rick held her hips, lifting them from the bed as he thrust up to meet her down stroke. She tightened around his cock, muscles locking him deep then milking his length. He didn't fight it, letting the electric sparks free. The nerves lighted from his balls to his brain, then retraced the track to explode through his cock, so heavenly constricted in her sleek passage. Muscles engulfed him in undulating spasms.

The first wave of pressure exploded from his dick, locking his jaw. His Drakken pressed close then roared in his mind when Manny found her fangs and pierced the flesh over his heart. The echo of an answering trumpet, her female, filled his head as his body emptied, drained. He closed his eyes, exhaustion waiting to claim him.

Get up and take care of her. She's likely sore and will chill.

"I'm on it, lizard." He growled to the Drakken. "Let me enjoy a bit of time with her. *People* like to cuddle." Ignoring his own retort, he rolled Manny to the bed and pulled the comforter over her for warmth. "Not that she needs it, she's burning up."

He got out of bed, checked a last time to make sure she was okay. Assured, he went into the connected bathroom, dropped the condom into the trash, and cleaned up. Looking in the mirror, he found the bite she left. The holes still trickled a bit of blood. Holding tissue to the wound sure it would clot shortly, he dampened a towel for her.

Beside her at the bed, he wiped the blood off her chin, and swept the towel over her face and body. She moaned and he paused but she didn't wake. He tossed the towels into the laundry and checked on her again.

She slept deeply as if she hadn't been sleeping well. He hated to disturb her, but he was dragging on his last reserve, too. Opening the window to the night, he pulled back the covers. Rick gathered her in his arms, her slight body draped between his elbows. She seemed so much bigger, more intimidating when she was awake. In his arms, tucked snug against his chest, she was softly feminine and petite in form.

He finally convinced his arms to put her in back in bed, moved in beside her and pulled the covers over both. His chest hurt when he moved, that was going to bruise. He smiled in the darkness and pulled Manny closer to his body. She found a comfortable position and sighed. Rick followed her to sleep.

***

Aware, the infant studied the people around him. The echo of a singular heartbeat was gone. It stopped before he entered the light. Scared at first, the infant relaxed as the welcome made up for it.

"A male child, already experiencing shifting capabilities."

The first voice he heard was not muffled. It was loud and

startling. He blushed at the coldness in the tone. The male kept speaking.

"Let's clean him up, start the testing."

He passed into a cradle of hands. This wasn't so bad. Then bright lights, fluid warmer than usual, and wrapping around his body so snug he couldn't move. His eyes were forced open and cold fluid dropped into them. He cried, but the female shushed him.

"How is he doing?" The head male again. The infant could tell from the tone of voice.

"He's reverted to flesh, the blue scaling faded. His eyes are human normal, no sign of the elongated pupil you asked us to look for." The nurse thought he was a perfect boy. He would never be a boy. He knew that much for certain. Not from his quick study of her mind.

Laurel lifted the infant from the nest and studied the baby. "I want to see some of that genetics you were bred to exhibit. I'll give you time." Laurel put the baby back into the bassinette. "Let me know of any changes."

The infant answered him, but he wasn't heard.

I heard you. BJ reached out, happy to find one close to his age. The other voice he'd been hearing in his head he didn't want to answer.

Hello. The infant repeated the word first used to him.

"Yes, doctor." The nurse watched him stride away. He paid good money. She didn't have all the information on why he was doing this research. Briefed on what to look for, she already knew obstetrics. She wouldn't consider the room behind her. Other staff were taking care of the body. This was her career now, being paid under the table for her expertise.

"How are you feeling, my dear?" Laurel looked over the chart of the second breeder he'd saved. She should be delivering within a week of the other.

"Wonderful, doctor. The baby is kicking and playing, I feel great."

"Good to hear." He closed the chart and smiled at her. "Not much longer and we'll have a baby to dote on."

"I am so excited." The woman smiled and rubbed her extended belly.

"So am I, dear." He walked out the door, making sure it locked behind him. "So am I."

***

There is a new one like me. He's just into the light. BJ told James the way he'd always communicated with his father.

James started, glanced up from the laptop he'd been studying. *You're sure? How about another one?*

Just the one. The man is with another mother. He says it'll be soon. James got to his feet, crossed to the travel crib where BJ played with his toes. He kissed the boy and pulled the phone from his pocket. Mitch would want to know this.

***

"Mitch, I found a lead on a missing nurse."

"I'm listening." He stopped what he was doing, holding the phone to his ear.

"The records we have indicate a birth soon, if not current. Laurel has no nursing staff. Fired from the premier hospital in Atlanta, she worked the neonatal unit. It happened two weeks ago. Her bank account sat empty for those two weeks, and then a deposit dropped."

"Unemployment?"

"Not this big a lump sum and not that quickly."

"How big?" Mitch stalked to the porch. Morning was late on this side of the mountain, but the sun was highlighting the pitch of the hill in front of him. He should have finished making the coffee."

"Five K and there have been one a week since then."

Mitch shook his head. "Not a federal fund."

"My money is on a generous endowment from our friend."

"You're sure?"

"I have the routing information. Unfortunately, it doesn't help me much with finding the physical address."

"She's from the Atlanta area, he's close by." Mitch sounded sure.

"So back to searching rental properties." Jake chuckled. "I think I'm going for my realtor's license when I'm done here."

"I'll pay for it. Keep me posted. I shudder to think what he's going to do with those infants."

"Sir."

"Morning." Arms wrapped Mitch's waist from behind. Regina

pressed against him in just her gown.

"Woman, did I not get you a robe?" There was love in the scold.

She smiled. "All I need is you to keep me warm."

Mitch took her down the hallway back to their room.

"I thought I heard something." James walked barefooted back to the kitchen.

"Mitch carried Reggie back to bed." Tracy rocked BJ as he nursed.

"Guess we have a few minutes until breakfast." He grinned suggestively at her.

"Good thing we took care of that last night," she teased him. He wasn't over the despair at her kidnapping. The proof was nightmares waking him in the night, the twitch of muscles unable to act on her rescue.

"Tell me there's coffee, lie to me if you must," Gareth growled into the room. His eyes squinted nearly shut, his feet bare as James', his gray hair hadn't seen a comb. He was shirtless and the pants he wore rode low over his hipbones.

"All you care to drink." James waved at the counter. A full carafe filled the air with aromatic perfume.

"Good enough." Gareth searched the cabinet for a cup, filled it with the brew and took his first hot and bitter sip. He growled low in his throat.

"Rough night?" Tracy watched him drink then exchanged a look with James.

"Could be worse." He emptied the cup and refilled it. "I guess I should make some more." He sipped and got busy. "You know what we need? A hot tub. Lots of space on the deck. Or even a heated pool. Swim a little of the stiffness out when we get back." The fragrance of fresh brew filled the air.

"I smell coffee." Mike groaned as he entered the kitchen. He paused by Gareth, taking a morning kiss before filling his cup. "Thank everyone who had a hand in this bracing potion, from the seeds that grew the trees to the hands that pulverized them this morning." He slid into the seat beside James. "How's BJ this morning?"

"He's doing fine. Just finished the first of his meals." James smiled at the burp.

"Good deal." Mike watched Gareth over the edge of his mug. "How are you doing?" Mike asked his mate.

Gareth finally opened his eyes, deep into his second cup of coffee. "I'm good." Hip rested against the edge of the counter.

"You took quite a spill last night."

"We agreed not to mention that."

Tracy took BJ from James and headed quickly from the growing confrontation. Even a teasing one could quickly escalate. She didn't want the baby around. BJ was alert, more than another infant. His Drakken soaked up the conversations going on around him.

James looked between the men, listening silently as usual. He'd been with them on practice last night. Gareth took a hard header into a tree, compliments of a limb that caught his wing tip he hadn't seen while making a tight turn. He'd gotten up and back into the air, but he had to hurt this morning.

"You're tight?" James asked when Gareth finally moved to sit beside Mike.

"All the way. The shift healed most of it. We're pretty hard to hurt."

"So, we saw." James nodded, filled his cup with fresh brew.

"So, breakfast?" Mike asked, eyes clear now and alert.

"Your choice." James told him with a big smile.

"Seriously?"

"You asked first. That means you make it. Same rules apply above as *Below*, remember?" He found a seat with a dry chuckle. He'd outfoxed the tech and enjoyed the return to the rare closeness they somehow missed after rescue. James respected the new team, but the bonds forged in blood and death were stronger.

"Wonder what's in the cabinets." Mike slipped out of the seat and started looking around.

CHAPTER 7

"I smell ham." Rick growled, voice husky with sleep.

"It's bacon." Manny told him on a yawn. She'd been first awake. The scent of coffee pulled her from deep slumber she hadn't enjoyed in months.

"Maybe both. Depends on who's cooking." He tossed aside the covers, moved to the side of the bed and took a moment to scrape his fingers through his already tousled hair. He got to his feet and walked to the bathroom.

Manny studied him in the natural light. Strong and rugged, her mate pleased her from head to toe. She started at the purr working through her chest. Blinking up at Rick when he backed out of the doorway, a flush filled her cheeks. "Sorry."

"About what? That little giveaway?" He moved to the bedside, sat, and trapped her in the covers.

"Um, yeah." She watched him like a mongoose staring down a cobra, his face coming closer until their lips met. All thoughts of embarrassment dissolved. The feminine creature under her skin flexed and Manny didn't hesitate to let her lead. In a sinuous twisting move, she pulled Rick to the mattress, pressing him down and moving over him. His cock already in the mood stood tall and hard from his body.

She lined them, careful to stay on the mattress with her knees. It wouldn't have mattered, scales, small yet toothed covered her knees and dug into the bedding, giving her traction.

"By the goddess, you are beautiful." Rick breathed as she took him deep.

Looking down at him then, she caught the glow of her eyes in his features. His hands were cool against her sides and she shivered. The same softer scales erupted over her body at his touch. She watched in fascination as they broke out down her arms. Her hands shifting form on his shoulders. Rich, iridescent aubergine coated her skin.

"Ride away, precious Pixie," Rick growled.

Her body tightened around his. His cock expanded to fill every inch of her. She licked her lips, or tried to make the movement and found her form changed completely. A rush of panic overtook the sexual craving and she straightened.

"No, Pixie. Don't go yet. Stay and play. You're perfect. Hang in there." Rick coaxed his mate, his voice a gravel echo of his smoother tones as human. He lifted her hips and the chafe of his flesh against tight muscles pulled her back into the maelstrom of emotions.

"I'm a kin." She didn't recognize the voice in her ears, the sound bigger than normal.

"You are a beautiful kin, Manny. I'll show you." Orange broke out over him. His eyes moved with surety into his Drakken gaze and locked with hers. He thrust deep and smiled when she gasped. He rolled her over, taking the lead. He pulled her legs around his hips, his form larger to match the increase in size of hers.

Manny gasped. Every sensation, every friction between them formed an erotic dance. Her kin strong, she stretched under her mate, the driving force of him. He was formidable. He held her close and moved deeply within, so deep again she curled against the pain. Her knees high, she clenched her teeth. Her arms held him close. Her heels beat against his back, urging him harder and faster with his strokes.

Before the storm took her, her orgasm rushing closer, she stiffened in real pain.

Rick slammed into the saddle of her body, holding still as possible while his lungs pumped for oxygen and his heart wobbled with the activity. His cock flexed, dragging a throttled moan from Manny's throat. His Drakken paused Rick's hips, taking in the situation.

Don't move. She will return the clasp in a moment.

What clasp? I'm causing her pain. My dick—

Is holding us deep to conceive, the Drakken explained with no small satisfaction.

I'm hurting her, you orange bastard. Rick stiffened, shifted his weight to pull back.

The Drakken inside his skin had more power in this shared form. Bipedal, the Drakken exposed the scales, the eyes, and the strength. His size was greater and he had no trouble subduing the human side of Rick to keep him deeply embedded in his mate. Satisfaction filled his mental instruction. *It is natural*.

Before Rick could answer, a vicious sting enveloped his cock from crown to balls. "Goddess damn, that hurts." Unable to pull against the pain he froze in place, his gaze on Manny's. She nodded but somehow kept from moving under him. He glanced between them to make sure she was still breathing.

Remain still.

As if I'd be able to move. The inner conversation halted and Rick cradled Manny close. Those expressive pink eyes hadn't blinked once.

"Pixie, you with me? The Drakken says this is natural. Hold still and it will pass."

"I'm so ready, Rick. So need to let go." The words delivered on wisps of breath, each one a stab in his chest cavity.

"It's going to hurt you, Pixie."

She took the lead with a small thrust, enough to stretch the scales or teeth or whatever covered their genitals. The orgasm rolled over her on the second controlled thrust and she pushed her head into the mattress as shudders moved over her, through her. Her belly rasped against Rick's. Her claws raked his back.

Rick clenched his teeth, every pointy tip meshed, smelling blood and helpless to do anything except hang over her while his cock shredded in her muscled hold. The scales along the length of his erection flexed, dragging him deeper into her body and he threw back his head with a roar to wake the dead.

Rick cradled Manny in his arms, the Drakken kin form dissolved and left behind sweaty and blood-smeared flesh. She smiled up at him. He brushed a stray lock of hair from her damp temple. An answering smile lifted his lips. "Are you okay?" His whisper was soft as the roar loud. He looked deeply into her eyes, daring her to lie to him one more time.

"I am healing as we speak." The slurp and smack of their bodies separating filled the silence. "I think I` should go clean up. If I know the boss, he's about five seconds from coming through that door." She tipped her head but didn't break eye contact.

Rick grabbed her hand, opened her fingers, and placed a kiss there. He closed his eyes for a moment and nodded. Keeping his lips pressed into the center.

Everything seems to be fine, Commander. We'll be down in a few minutes. He returned the answer along the same tight communication link used by Mitch. He held onto Manny's hand, following her from the bed.

There was blood smeared on both yet no injuries he could find as they showered together. Once they'd toweled off, it was as if nothing had happened.

She is the one mate. The Drakken sharing Rick's mind supplied with no small amount of satisfaction.

Did you have to hurt her? Rick dressed quickly, matching Manny's speed.

We did no injury to our mate. The Drakken's tone sounded miffed this time. As if even the suggestion was beyond imagination. *We consummated our union. We are mates, we belong to each other, we are one*.

"Consummated, huh?" Rick snorted aloud.

"Rick?" Manny stopped, looking over at him.

"Just trying to figure out what happened."

"I believe we took the last step." Manny stepped over to him. She watched him straighten from tying his boots. Hers were already knotted and ready for the day. Putting her hands on his hips, she pulled him the half-step to her. "We are mated Drakkens. I admit I wanted it a little slower, but it's done."

"Are you okay?" He didn't resist the need to wrap his arms around her, to hold her closer again.

"How many times do I have to answer that?" She smiled at him, leaning forward to touch forehead to forehead. "There was no condom in play with us. I might have a nervous moment or two about that." A glimmer of her Drakken flashed through her eyes. "I am fine. I feel better about all of this." Pulling back, she shrugged without releasing him. "I understand more of what's going on. All of this is natural, the scales, the blood." She moved to step away. "I don't know why the wait was so important to me." In her mind, her creature snorted.

Of course, you know. This is nothing. Any male would take you as he has. The real test is to come. The voice hardened. *He'll have to best me to have me*. Manny shuddered, the voice unheard by anyone but her.

Rick pulled her against his chest, stopping the retreat. The slow double beat of his heart under her ear soothed her and steadied her heart to match his rhythm. "I didn't know that would happen, never guessed it could happen." He pushed her back. "I am sorry to hurt you."

"That is why we have the healing, Rick. Or so I believe. These things are likely a mechanism to keep us bound together for the mating plunge that Tracy talked about." The thought of locking genitals with Rick and then free falling back to earth scared her more than she could admit.

CHAPTER 8

"You've been thinking hard about the Drakken."

Manny shrugged. "It was inevitable, no matter how hard I fought. I am glad it was you, Rick." There was more she wanted to say and needed him to hear. A knock on the door reminded them of the current situation.

"C'mon, you guys. We want to hear what happened."

Rick smiled at the stage whisper. Tracy, their cheerleader, their little sister, the one *Below* that kept them human had sneaked upstairs. Her impatience had her hand in mid-knock when Rick opened the door.

"Nosey."

"Curious." Tracy never hesitated, throwing her arms around his waist, and hugging close.

"Don't let Jimmy see you do that. He'll threaten to beat my ass." Rick studied her, seeing the secret in her eyes. "You know about this, don't you?" He glanced over her shoulder, but the landing behind her was empty. He'd have put the question to James had his brother been standing there. Rick would bet James and Tracy had experienced what he and Manny'd just gone through.

Tracy bit her lip, glancing away.

"Trace, I'm warning you." Rick shook her once, clutching her shoulders.

"Rick, stop. We can talk this over with Regina. She's the resident expert." Manny pushed past them and headed downstairs in a silent glide that drew Rick's gaze.

Manny had to move. The sight of the other woman's arms

around her mate disturbed her. Primitive thoughts of death and the hard spirit of jealousy twined and urged Manny to strike. She never looked back, taking her confusion and sudden anger downstairs quickly.

He could watch her move forever. His Drakken tried to explain something but he didn't listen.

"She's right, Rick." Tracy pulled away and followed Manny. "Let's talk with Reggie."

Bemused, he headed down last.

The kitchen was a noisy safe zone, everyone filled plates from the counter and stove before sitting down. In the atmosphere redolent of coffee and the sweetness of maple syrup, male voices bounced from wall to wall. A short silence fell as soon as Manny's foot crossed from hardwood to tile. Then it resumed as they welcomed a teammate into breakfast.

"Mike cooked bacon, ham, cheese omelets, pancakes and biscuits and gravy." Regina told her as she passed with a plate. "There's coffee and hot water for tea." She nodded and slipped into her seat beside Mitch.

Manny glanced at her boss holding a soft conversation with James to his right. Tracy pushed past Manny with Rick in tow then left him at the door to sit with her mate. Mike and Gareth didn't look at her at all. Instead, they fixed concerned gazes on Rick when he stopped at the door.

"Morning." Rick told the room in general, nodding at Mitch then joining Manny. The chorus answering him ranged in tone from friendly to guarded. His stomach clenched. He'd really announced the relationship this time. What a fuck up.

"You both doing okay?" Unable to stop himself, Mike moved beside them, taking a warm tray of bacon from the oven as an excuse.

"Fine." Manny told him, taking her coffee to the open end of the table. She left the end seat to Rick, sitting across from Gareth.

"No complaints." Rick filled a plate without looking at them, wanting to get this over, yet stalling.

He took his seat, only then noticing the piles of food on his plate.

"You must be hungry," Manny told him, taking delicate bites of light and fluffy biscuits covered in red-eye gravy.

"I think so," Rick answered her yet kept his gaze on the plate.

Conversation dribbled to a halt. Silence grew until Manny couldn't swallow. She picked up the coffee cup and warmed suddenly cold fingers around the outside. Sipping the brew, she managed to clear the obstruction in her throat. She'd just put the cup down and moved her hands to her lap when the boss started the interrogation.

"Something you want to say?" Mitch asked across the table, bringing Rick's head up to meet his commander's steady and encouraging gaze.

"It's complicated." He glanced at Manny. No help there. A soft rosy blush colored her tanned skin and he reached for her hand under the table.

"Somehow, I think it's old news." Mitch leaned back in his chair. "Let us decide."

Manny squeezed his hand under the table, lending him silent support. Uncomfortable, her newly freed Drakken growled and paced, ready to strike out in defense. It was weird for Manny to be on the cooler side of the emotional creature. Normally Manny was the one pacing and fretting.

"Meet the newest mates." Rick's smile half slipped off his face. *Epic fail*. No one rushed to fill the silence. The image a bomb fuse in the last seconds fizzled in his mind's eye.

"About time you recognized that fact." Smiling at Manny instead of looking at Rick, Regina patted Manny's shoulder.

"We're not done." Manny told her. The biscuit she'd eaten churned with determination set on violent freedom.

"It's a start," Regina assured her.

Rick's hand in hers under the table tightened in brutal assertion and the biscuit began to settle. Manny managed a full breath.

"There's a physical issue with the Drakken." Rick glanced at Mike and Gareth.

"We know something about that." James, the quietest one of the group, offered. "Experienced it not long ago."

"What's going on?" Gareth filled the looming silence.

"I meant to ask Regina." Rick nodded his head in her direction, gaze meeting hers.

Mitch turned to her. "We haven't experienced it, not that I

know of."

"You'd know." Rick nodded along with James.

"What is it?" Regina pushed her chair back a bit to see both couples. James deferred to Rick.

"Manny took form as the kin." He paused, remembering how magnificent she had been. He lifted her hand and kissed her knuckles slowly and suggestively. "Beautiful girl." He took a deep breath, gathering his words. "In form -- having sex -- something happened."

At this pause, James spoke out.

"Scales developed between us, intimately digging into softer flesh. It didn't happen the first time we had sex or times after that. This last time," he added.

"Scales?" Regina's gaze turned inward, seeking an answer. She really needed to catch up on some courses. Being an archaeological linguist focused on ancient script wasn't cutting the biology she needed.

In the last few years she'd nursed shell-shocked men back into their human minds, while helping them adjust to the new forms they'd all received from the injections she'd thought safe. The next generation of soldiers filled her kitchen, not all of them but most, and she understood so little of their secondary biology.

"I believe, from what Tracy shared—" Manny stopped when Regina's head snapped upright, those blue eyes fastening on her laser sharp.

"Listening."

"Um, the mating plummet, maybe it's to help that." Clammy, her handhold with Rick slipped a little and she grasped him harder. By the tingles she knew she'd cut off circulation but she had no desire to break their hold. "The climb is very high and the clasp, like other lizards, maybe..." She finished with a shrug. Biology wasn't her strong suit. She liked chemistry and knowing how to blow things up.

"Good thinking. You might be on to something." Regina turned to Mitch, who shrugged and looked baffled.

"No idea. Sounds like a reasonable explanation, though."

"Oh, by all the hells, no!" Mike pushed away from Gareth and the table. "I'm never flying with you again. Not gonna tear me up."

"I don't think you'll have an issue." Standing unnoticed in the doorway, Ben reassured Mike. “The guardians accept you both as a power couple, not a mating couple. Yet. So there should be no chance of that happening between you, in flight or not.”

“Come in, Ben. Breakfast?” Mitch turned his phone face down. He’d gotten the alert that someone had crossed into his territory an hour ago. Not long after that he’d ended his call with Jake.

“Are you sure?” Gareth stood next to Mike, his greater size a comfort to his mate.

“As of the last we spoke, yes. You need not fear the scaled clasp, as it were.” He sniffed deeply and smiled. “That all smells so good. I’m starved.” He wasted no time filling a plate and grabbed the free seat between Manny and Regina. Tucking into the warm food, he didn’t speak again until he cleaned the plate and finished a cup of coffee. “That is a long, hungry trek up here.”

By that time, Mike and Gareth had left the room. BJ was awake again and ready for feeding, so Tracy was missing. Manny nursed her third cup of coffee, as silent as James was across the table. Rick and Mitch were talking business.

“This is a biological imperative due to the mating flight?” Regina asked Ben as he pushed the plate away with a satisfied grunt. She’d turned the idea over in her mind, wondering why she and Mitch hadn’t experienced the act.

“So far as I can tell. It’s new and only between mating couples.”

“Why haven’t we gone through it?” Regina asked, looking from Ben to Mitch. Mitch shrugged and nodded toward Ben.

“Don’t ask me. Maybe, due to your delay in taking form or your injuries, the body wasn’t ready for mating.”

His simple words were of much more import. Regina had nearly died and was hanging onto life by a thread when Mitch rescued her. His Drakken, a form he was familiar with, took her to mate and healed her as he knew how, by sex. A new woman woke from their post-coital nap, still frail looking, still pounds underweight, but with energy and renewed fire for life.

“Okay, then.” Regina clapped her hands. “As far as we know, it’s happened twice, once to each of you.” She watched James for his slow nod and leaned across Ben to see Rick and Manny nod. “Then until we have a better sampling, I’m guessing you know what to expect. Maybe not every time but certainly when the spirit moves."

"That's my best guess." Ben stood with his plate. "I'll dry if someone volunteers to wash." He moved to the sink and the rest of the dirty dishes.

"We'll load the dishwasher." Regina told him with another telling look at Mitch. "Somehow I think you have business to discuss." She got to her feet with more dishes in hand.

"Busted." Ben smiled at her and filled a cup with water, dunking two tea bags of green tea. "Whenever you're ready, boss."

Mitch rose and stepped to Regina's side to refill his coffee. He pulled her close, smelling her shampoo and her velvety vanilla scent, and kissed the top of her head. "Don't let us work through lunch."

"Promise." She didn't turn to watch him leave but turned to the task ahead.

CHAPTER 9

"Let us get these, Regina. You rest or research or whatever you want to do," Manny insisted. She needed to be busy at something. She feared downtime would have her back in bed with Rick, exploring every facet of her new self.

"If you're sure."

At Rick's nod, she smiled and wiped her hands dry. "Thank you both." She left, her mind already adding the latest information to the growing stockpile of knowledge on the Drakken race.

"Are you avoiding me?" Rick's question came from deep in his chest. His voice was an intriguing combination of man and animal. Manny loved the timbre of them together. The beast so close to the surface in him was a true partner in the grand scheme of things.

"Not at all. I'm here with you in the kitchen, just doing chores." Manny stacked the dishes like cards, and stood the silver upright in the holder. The little bit of domesticity drew her from the worry of her future. She wasn't a sharer by nature.

"Hey, Pixie." His voice dropped to a lower register, her Drakken immediately sat up and took notice.

"Rick?" Manny washed her hands, letting bubbles grow. She stalled as long as possible. She knew he wanted to talk. Since she'd been raised by her father, talking casual conversation wasn't customary for her. Girlfriends chatted, they discussed feelings and dresses and boyfriends. Manny had never had that growing up. Later, the competition for what she wanted was so fierce there were no girlfriends.

"I need you with me, Manuela."

The Drakken in her agreed. Rushing to dry her hands, Manny mentally stroked the creature. Regina was right. The smaller form was not a bruiser. Yet she could hold her own in a fight. Never forget that. Still, the Drakken was entirely feminine in ways even human females couldn't achieve.

She finished drying her hands and closed the dishwasher then listened as it filled. She gave in to his plea because she wanted to. "Yes, Rick." She turned to face him in time for him to plant a kiss on her lips. He didn't move, except to turn her fully to his chest. He wrapped his arms around her to hold her still.

With her arms trapped between them, Manny stiffened then relaxed. He wouldn't hurt her. She knew this deep down inside. Yet, it continued to be a struggle to let him have his way, to let Rick direct time between them. Her lips responded, parting just enough to release a small moan. The sound and breath braided into a sexual catalyst. Never breaking contact, he loosened his hold around her and in a moment swept her into the cradle of his arms.

Her arms wrapped around his neck, eyes closed, trusting him. Always in the back of her mind, no matter what was happening, she worked feverishly on the methods she'd need to release herself and get into a fighting stance.

A hard twist and she'd drop, going low. Crouching, she would sweep out her leg, taking him down. A jump over his prone body and one stomp to his shoulder, breaking it or dislocating it, a knee to his ribs, knife across his throat. Well done, she congratulated herself. Her feet hit the floor. The kiss was broken.

"Are you serious?" Rick leaned over her. He put both hands on the counter he'd trapped her against. He touched her nose with his. "I'm setting up a seduction and you're planning an attack?"

Manny took a moment to gather her wits. She'd always compartmentalized mentally. It kept her emotions in check, her rational mind sharp, aware. She hadn't always thought that way, not as a child or a young adult. Thinking back now, she wasn't sure when it started. Her first enlistment, or maybe sometime later, training for her first mercenary job.

This is the part of her that Rick and his over-confident Drakken would have to overcome. He'd have to sway her with his strength, prove he could overtake her, master her without breaking her. The very thought of him mastering her gave her chills. Yet as it rooted in her mind, the warmth of what could be overtook it. He would prove his mastery over her. When they were airborne he'd take her, claiming her after an aerial battle of epic proportions.

Confused, Manny felt her emotions tumble in an uncontrollable maelstrom. One thought fought free of the jumble, she needed freedom. Flight was her best option. Fear took her control. Manny ducked under his arm and lunged for the front door. Thank all hells it was open. She leaped down the steps and tore into the late morning. Her Drakken kin pushed for release. Manny used a mental choke hold to keep her bottled inside. She had to think about this, more again fully. She wasn't strong enough to face this part of mating. Not yet. Not with Rick.

In a nutshell, the statement was a microcosm of their relationship. He wanted the seduction, she needed the fight, the upper hand.

Pictures, snap shots really, flashed through her head as she moved in full retreat. She watched the air dancers, saw the mating clasp, the plummet. Every cell in her body cried out for the fulfillment she craved. Need wasn't a strong enough word for what filled her for Rick. Her Drakken roared in her mind, shaking her brain, total punishment. Her lips sealed, Manny clasped her hands over her ears to muffle the noise. She dodged the sunlight and slipped into the woods where the shadows chilled her body until the creature adjusted her temperature.

Rick watched her go, trying to follow her train of thought, a jumbled mass of contradictions until the last. Floored she wanted that from him, that she needed that. He didn't know what to do. He couldn't follow her, not until he'd digested what she'd admitted in her heart. He understood on the surface and more, now that she'd actually blown open her own mind. He'd caught every nuance, every contrary emotion and thought.

"What is it this time?" Gareth, still dressed in sleep pants and barefoot, pushed past Rick in the doorway.

"She planned a takedown while I was kissing her." Rick ran a hand through his hair. Fuck all, he'd opened his mouth before he could stop the thought. He was going to have to install better filters.

"You picked a wild one, Carlisle. No doubt." Gareth opened the freezer and lifted his glass. He dropped several ice cubes in his drink then turned to face his teammate. “Can you handle it?” He sipped and watched Rick.

Rick shook his head, turning back to take a seat at the clean table. “Gods’ balls.” He looked over where Gareth leaned against the counter. “I never expected or even suspected.”

“It’s a wild world out there, bro. We make it wilder by the minute. Drakken are a primal breed. Their needs are a force we never faced.” He sipped the icy water. “These creatures are simple and strong. You know that from *Below*.” A silence fell while their minds turned to life when it was minute to minute and three people struggled to lead them back to their sanity.

“I get it, but this is part of the woman.” Rick snapped the memory thread. His elbows rested on his knees. His hands clasped tightly. “Manny is made of diverse parts, and the Drakken is creating more fractures.” He tried to explain to Gareth.

Concerned now, Gareth took a seat beside him. The solid thunk of his glass on the table served to underscore to the sudden anxiety. “She’s okay, right? You’re mated and all that foolishness?”

“I thought we were through with all that.” Rick shrugged. His glance moved to follow his mate. “She’s always got a guard up. She always plans an escape, an attack, a defense. She’s lived like that for so long.” He looked up at Gareth, locked gazes his full of despair. “I wonder if she’ll be able to change.”

***

Laurel smiled into the glass. Two infants rested with tummies full. The bodies of the breeders were gone. Everything had been sanitized. The initial blood draws of the infants were inconclusive, yet as he watched the nurse approach them the first born kicked, his bare legs showing an instant of blue snakeskin.

Laurel frowned. He worried for a moment, then he assured himself the infant didn’t need scales, not yet. It was possible they didn’t achieve the harder protection until puberty. Laurel had plenty of time. Waiting wasn’t an issue, but these blood tests would tell him much earlier if what he theorized was correct.

He could breed these creatures, the next gen soldiers the world would pay top dollar to own. They’d undergo conditioning and training, and of course there would be schooling. He didn’t want to turn them over as infants. Whatever would the military do with them? The same thing Laurel wanted to do, test them over and over to see where their abilities stopped. Push them until they fell in their tracks to test their strength. If they could fly…

The boy woke then, his chest flared a pastel berry shade, almost the color of ripe strawberries in the light. Yes, his breeders were true and the amazing Jenkins had not been wrong. He didn't spare another thought for his dead assistant.

I'm cold.

They'll be by to cover you again. I hear footsteps. The first boy child spoke to the new male, and by listening in on conversations and repeating the words in order, he'd also spoken with BJ.

BJ chimed in. *In time you'll be able to regulate your temperature.* He tried to keep the mental path hidden from the older voice. That one he didn't know or trust. There were many blocked pathways in the mind of that one. He hadn't yet thought to give the information to his parents.

"Dr. Laurel." The dulcet tones of one of the twins pulled Laurel's attention away from the infants.

"What is it?"

"We ran the comparisons you asked for. In a tech trial your theory holds soundly." She offered him papers. The neat, handwritten script was easy enough to read and filled him with excitement. He scanned the data and checked the math. Senoia Knyght watched him check her findings. She and her brother, fraternal twins, worked best side by side.

"Wonderful. Now we need to start the next set of trials." Laurel turned to walk down the hallway. She followed him silently. He so appreciated that. He appreciated both after recently testing them out of the lab.

They'd fallen into bed with him as quickly as Jenkins had. He loved the added sexual power he held over them, the way they strove to please him. Anything he'd wanted to try, they'd participated in whole heartedly. Their minds and bodies a pleasure, the Knyght twins were his perfect duo. He decided to keep them, make them rich and tie them to him just as he'd tried to tie the traitor Regina. His mood darkening, he paused in the lab to don his coat.

CHAPTER 10

Manny stumbled and fell full length, her foot trapped on the other side of a small fallen tree. Her ankle didn't hurt, so she tugged it free and rolled to her back. Only then did she notice the tracks of moisture on her face. Her chest rose and fell with the need for air. Her double heartbeat throbbed against her ribs.

She wiped her cheeks dry, took a deep breath and let the kin form have some freedom. Her jeans tightened around her waist and she hurried to unfasten them. There, much better. In deep shadow, where trees were so close together the early spring leaves blocked out the sunlight, she stared up. In this form she connected with her other half readily.

What has happened?

"He wants to take the dive." Manny sniffed, letting the mental exhaustion press her into the ground.

So that is what you do.

"It is not what we do." Manny pushed up on her hands. She stared at the toes of her boots, scuffed and dirty. They needed to come off. She started working on the laces, her fingers clumsy at best.

Why do you not want to mate your mate?

Why did she have to sound so reasonable? How was Manny to clarify something that the Drakken already knew? She kicked off her boot and slipped the sock off.

That feels nice.

Manny curled her lip. She attacked the other boot, toed it off and rolled her socks up before she stuffed them in the boots. Manny flopped back to the ground, letting the earth embrace her.

The weight of her concerns seemed less.

"I want to mate him, but it's going to be dangerous."

You mean he must dominate you. There is always danger.

"You were created out of left-over and scrambled DNA. What do you know about it?" At Manny's challenge, the Drakken flexed. She quickly scrambled out of the rest of her clothes. Mitch warned them all not to shift in daylight, but if she'd angered the creature there would be no clothes to wear home.

I come from ancient times. I existed on this place long before your ancestors were born. My DNA is pure and has always been so. There is no muddling of my species. Disdain filled the voice, then the female preened and scales erupted over Manny's body.

Manny piled her clothes and wondered if she could hide thoughts from the Drakken.

No, you cannot hide from me.

Manny's anger bloomed, hot and powerful. The confluence of the Drakken's superior tone and the rush of Manny's emotional storm blasted her from her anchor. The small clearing blew outward with the explosive shift of form. Manny shook her head, dazed at the rush of power that filled her. Air, her element of air pushed away the young vines, tore newly born leaves from limbs.

Her thoughts cleared somewhat and she looked through eyes not her own. The forest shades of green took on a three-dimensional focus. The colors were deeper, richer. She reached out to touch a leaf. The sight of her clawed hand covered in rich wine colors, the fingers tipped with pointed nails long enough to gut a grizzly bear, distracted her. She closed her fist with a mental command and watched the hand contract.

Opening her fingers, she reached for the leaf again. With her depth perception struggling to equalize itself, she managed to grasp the fragile foliage. She pulled it loose of the branch. At once the scent of sap wreathed her head. Manny snorted and lifted her gaze again. Her tail twitched when the command to walk forward broadcast through her body. Her wings, yes those were hers, stretched beside her in the clearing. She flexed them, feeling the membranes giving against the trunks of the trees.

This is all you are, Manuela. The self-satisfied voice filled her mind.

This is more. I don't know if I can hold back, if I can protect him.

You want to protect him? Why on earth would you do that? To have a mate to one such as we are is both a task and a treasure. He will understand this.

Not if I kill him before we can come to a compromise. Manny turned in a slow circle. So far she hadn't miss-stepped, hadn't tripped or fallen on her face. She considered it a win-win.

There will be no compromise. The voice in her head huffed and Manny watched the sapling she faced lean over. *Oh, that. You belong to the element of air, should anyone ask.* The Drakken took a few steps. *Yes, the compromising. He has no choice. If he commits to us, he will have to play to his strengths to take us. You have a fighting spirit, one that has been honed in fires only I know you've faced throughout your life. We need a mate, a male more than capable of taking care of us. There will be times only he will stand between us and our enemies. We must not simply trust he'll be there. We must know he is strong enough to defend and protect.*

The voice rang in Manny's head. She'd have to work on volume control. Still, she thought about what the Drakken told her. She wasn't wrong. Manny hesitated to commit to him because she'd been so strong for so long. Being dependent on another person went against her soul. She harbored the fear that he'd let her down. She'd been on her own before. She'd finished rigorous training, taken it farther into the Rangers and then had been the outsider as one of the few women who'd made it through.

Again, other men told her she didn't belong in the military. There'd been hints and accusations both behind her back and to her face. Men, her teammates, her army company, brothers-in-arms, called her choice names and berated her much as her father had. All the resentment she'd had to keep inside. The anger had fed on her until nothing lived inside of Manuela. She'd morphed into nicknames, some of them nice, some not. She'd been useful in EOD where her team had to depend on her for their safety.

He… What could she say to the Drakken who seemed so confident in their mate? What possible argument could Manny use to convince the female who shared her skin this wasn't going to work. That this dream of having Rick was doomed to failure.

There have been enough arguments on this subject. One night soon we will take wing. The Drakken interjected the last, stopping any further conversation.

Manny couldn't ignore the wistful tone in the order. She had no doubt her wild half wanted to fly. Together they stared at the canopy of green that separated them from the last step. Together they sighed and Manny felt another chunk of her resistance falling away. That same longing wove through her body as well as in the scaled giant balanced on four legs.

We cannot fly until the sun sets. That is an order.

I know, but this feels so much like freedom, so much the way I should be in my existence.

How about we practice the walking and not falling over. Manny directed her front leg to move forward. It moved, but her other legs remained steady and planted on the ground. *I think you're going to have to help me.* She snorted at her mental roommate.

Then pay attention. Manny relaxed somewhat, a new feeling for her as she allowed the Drakken space inside her head. *It's a matter of balance. Once we take to the air it will be easier for you.* She started them walking at a slow pace.

Manny studied the weight shift and confidently slipped behind the driver's wheel in her mind about the third trip around the clearing. The Drakken let her take over but hovered at the edge, watching her human assume control.

Manny picked up the pace from stroll to trot, the weight distribution settling into a rhythm in her mind. Her confidence grew with her speed and soon she was running. There would be no stumbling around on a landing for her. The Drakken approved.

Manny slowed and came to a stop, tired from working huge muscles in concert. She'd bolted without much breakfast and her belly reminded her with a loud growl. The last thing in the world she wanted to do is go back to that house and face Rick.

You need sustenance. There is food at the cabin. The Drakken deserted Manny.

Strength ripped from her muscles. Manny hit the ground, hands and knees splayed to catch her weight. Her arms quivered and she let go, falling full length a second time along the churned forest floor. She moaned and let her eyes slip closed. She knew she had to dress and get off the cushion of leaves and pine straw. The effort seemed Herculean and she let her body sink in deeper, nestling in the loam.

She didn't have the energy to yawn. Clothing or at least a weapon was crucial. Survival forced her to push up to hands and knees and make her way to her clothes. With her hand wrapped around the hilt of a knife, she gave in to the exhaustion that continued to suck her consciousness away.

You have no worry, Manuela. I am the weapon you will always have.

***

Rick finished cleaning the kitchen with Gareth's help, his mind stuck on Manny. The conundrum wasn't close to fixing itself and for some reason the other half of his partnership kept silent. He moved to the porch, then walked around the house when the swing evoked too many recent memories.

When there was still no sign of Manny and his Drakken started noticing the absence, he headed in the direction he'd seen her flee. The day wasn't far advanced, the sun warm on his shoulders. Over the peaks he watched clouds form. There'd be storms this afternoon.

Better they hold off until nightfall. Love the feel of rain on my scales.

"With my luck, you'd be struck by lightning." Rick pushed through bushes into the shade of the tree line. He stopped, the scent of his mate filled the clearing. Rick gazed around the area but didn't see her at first. He moved forward, casting about with gaze and scent, trying to pinpoint her.

The fallen tree hid her. In an instant, he'd leaped the trunk. Going to his knees beside her he touched her. There were no marks on her skin, the flesh smooth. He saw the lines on her back where a swimsuit top rested, the skin lighter in shade. Lower, the lighter skin made a tight T just above the curve of her cheeks.

"Manuela, honey—"

At the first syllable, she startled. He didn't see the knife until it glinted in the sunlight through the canopy. Manny rolled, the blade a swift strike hitting flesh and cutting through it with razor sharpness. She got to her feet, blinking the sleep from brain and body.

CHAPTER 11

Rick looked up at her, one hand outstretched to touch her, the other he lifted to hold his belly. The shirt beneath it was steadily soaking with his blood. "Gods damn it, Rick, shift forms." Manny didn't know where the directive came from, just that she had to tell him.

Rick didn't yet feel the cut. It would be a moment before his nerve endings flashed the information to his brain. Manny kept her knife sharp enough to cut air. He remained in place, watching her move in ways he'd seen before but not like this. This was through a mate's eyes. It appreciated the sinuous muscles that played across her body. She hunched over, her knife held ready as if to attack him again. His lips tipped in a smile. Manuela, his warrior.

"You are so beautiful." He lifted his hand and it seemed only then he noticed the blood. The growls resounding through his skull started making sense. He looked down, seeing the damage she'd done in less than a second. Rick chuckled and let the kin form loose. He'd been naked before. The greater size remained hampered by the boots and the jeans. Rick took care of the jeans with a hooked claw. The boots crushed his feet and took longer. He moved to his haunches and sliced the laces on the first boot.

"Fucker hurts," he growled. Then he leaned back with more respect as Manny sliced through the second set of laces. He kicked them free and sighed.

Not finished. The voice in his head gave just the short warning before taking to full size. *Want my mate, now*.

Manny stumbled back again, only to find the chair-sized claw wrapped around her. "Rick." The one word was a caution.

Mate. The female Drakken lifted her head in interest. *Don't fight it, Manuela.*

"Nobody calls me that." But the wail fell on deaf ears. She had a split second to think about how Regina felt when Manny *ma'am*ed her. Then biology took over and her Drakken resumed the winged form. She stumbled this time. The sheer size-change left her brain behind.

Blood thickened the air of the clearing and she bent low to look for the cut on Rick's belly. Nothing. Rick straightened, neck arched and wings out to his sides. He took up all the room in the clearing.

You know Mitch said not in daylight.

There's going to be an ass chewing when I get back. Rick's voice carried straight to her mind. He'd recovered from her attack and was his normal self. *Let's go. The sooner we get this over with the sooner we can move ahead.*

Not on your life. I'm not bucking the boss because you have some macho idea we need to fill the daytime skies. Manny stepped back. Her wings she kept folded, even though the Drakken wanted to unfurl and wing her way into the clouds.

It's biological. It's what comes next, Manuela.

Stop calling me that. I'm Manny or even Cox. Two snorts punctuated her statement. Both Drakken disagreed. Manny recalled then that her Drakken had referred to her in her full name. For fuck's sake, gods help her if the Drakken learned all of them.

Follow me. Rick started to back out of the clearing.

Manny had a second before his ass met the sunshine. Not hesitating, she unfurled her wings and asked the breeze to stop his escape. The trees and bushes behind him tightened to keep him imprisoned. Limbs wove in on each other, forming a solid green gate. When his backward motion stopped Rick's great orange head turned to her. The long slits in his eyes narrowed further. The challenge was clear. The moment seemed to be now. Manny wasn't sure she could do this. Hell, she'd nearly butchered him because she was still groggy from another deep sleep in less than a day.

Mitch. Said. No. Had she overreacted? No, of course she hadn't. She was toeing the line set by those who knew more about this situation than she did. It was her responsibility. The breeze, wind, hurricane she'd produced enclosed them. The inside of the clearing trembled inside the whirlwind.

I said let's go.

The growl was back and scary to hear. She'd faced down too many others bent on intimidating her. *I said no*. That was her line in the sand. *Until those scales disappear we're not going anywhere*. She had to clench her teeth and the magick swirling around her pushed her Drakken's patience. She wanted to mate, longed to join her mate. Manny held her tightly in check with sheer determination.

Rick moved toward her, his wings dropped low. His head stretched toward her on his lean neck, his muzzle parted and she could see his teeth.

I'm not afraid of you. Manny wasn't. Fear of him attacking didn't bother her one bit. What did bother her was the chance of discovery and the spike that settled in her chest that this is the moment when she'd lose him forever.

Rick, there is plenty of time for this. Manny tipped her chin, her head high, eyes as big as basketballs watched his every movement as he stalked her. No other word for it, he paced slowly across the already too small clearing to meet her.

I want you now. The growl of the Drakken told her the creature had full control. If she wanted to keep him at arm's length until both were ready, the fight could be epic --not what she wanted on this spring afternoon, not Armageddon, not with Rick.

The standoff froze in place. She stared at him mere inches away. His nostrils flared, his eyes lit from within with the chaos of needs and wants all tangled. She knew her eyes would resemble the glow in his. With everything in her she wanted to throw caution to the wind and take off with him. She wanted to experience all that he offered. Yet orders were orders, and she had to follow them to the letter. The training went bone deep, maybe soul deep. She'd been taught the chain of command until she could follow nothing else.

She might refer to Mitch as her boss, but the retired Naval Commander was her commanding officer. Rick knew this. Things flew through her mind so quickly she didn't have time to decipher them. Soundbites of her father, of Mitch, of Rick, the men in her life who meant something to her. This male stood before her, ready to trumpet a call to his female, a cry to bring her to heel.

Taking a chance, Manny forced the Drakken back from the forefront of her brain and let the huge purple form fade into fragile flesh. She fought the stagger at the change. Manny stood before Rick, her shoulders stiff and her chin jutted. The winds died down. Leaves and detritus settled to the ground. She left him with two choices. Then she removed one of those. He would not take her in form, not in this mental state. He would not mate her until she was ready. A shiver moved over her and chill bumps broke out along her limbs. Would she ever be ready?

Rick shook his head as his mate refused him her Drakken, taking the human form in front of his disbelieving eyes. The denial angered him, stirred his passion to primal levels he fought to control. He wanted to blast her, to lash out at her disobedience. He glared at her.

A soldier, she stood clothed in nothing but her belief, her staunch belief in following orders. She clung to guidelines she didn't need any longer. She ruled the very top of a permanently wrecked food chain. How could she not know this? He stomped in irritation because at the very heart of his anger love remained a steady flame in his heart.

He had no choice, which rubbed him wrong. He'd allowed her to best him. *That is what females do, my friend.* His Drakken explained. *We must love them and take care of them.* The resignation in his voice touched the core of wrath in Rick.

Allowing the Drakken control, Rick morphed back to human. He stared at her across the few feet separating them. He rubbed his hand across the echo of pain that burned his stomach. The cut was gone. Not even a red line remained. He held his hand out to Manny, fully expecting her to rebuff him again. She trembled across from him, yet her gaze told him nothing.

"Man— Pixie, love."

She couldn't stop the rush to touch him, to let him hold her now the maelstrom of emotions waned. She pressed close, hugged harder. Her throat constricted with tears she refused to shed. Even had she wanted to speak, the words created a gridlock between her brain and her lips.

"It's okay." Rick soothed her, his arms around her and her body pressed tightly against him.

Is it? That voice inside Rick's head, the one who fought the Drakken inserted. *She doesn't want anything to do with you. And here you are holding her, letting her get away with rejecting you, us, again. She's going to push us away again and you're going to let her. You don't want to force her to your will.*

Though Rick tried to ignore the voice, his emotions seemed to realize the truth. Rick had never been one quick to anger, yet the burn inside of him had existed for some time. He didn't realize it until brought to his attention. As if then he couldn't ignore it, the memories of how often she'd pushed him away surfaced, how she'd avoided being alone with him, how she'd danced and kept him dangling incited the fury.

His Drakken tired of the fight. His human spirit had taken one too many attacks. Rick snapped. He'd held onto his patience through everything to give her time to come to him. Rebuffed again, the animal side of his brain, stronger now with his female at hand, rebelled.

He pushed her away. Glaring into her face, he watched the frozen expression fade, leaving a dazed and confused regard in her eyes. "What is it going to take until you come to me? You know we belong together."

CHAPTER 12

Manny took a few steps back. Rick was angry, that was easy to see. The tone of his voice dropped but it didn't sound like the Drakken behind the question. She opened her mouth to...

There was nothing more to say. She'd told him. Hadn't she tried to keep him at arm's length until she could adjust to the Drakken? She needed time to adjust to the incredible mental challenge of sharing her thoughts with another entity. She needed time to come to terms with the wounds her upbringing left on her psyche.

"I need time." Manny hadn't realized she'd spoken the three words aloud until they filled the air with heat and heaviness that collapsed her lungs. She lifted her arms to cover her chest, perhaps to restart her heart, perhaps to add another layer of protection for the organ beating inside. She watched Rick turn and gather his clothing. He didn't look back when he left the clearing.

Manny went to her knees. The keening sound from the Drakken grew in her mind, making her clench her teeth. "Just shut up for a moment, please." Manny didn't recognize her voice at all. What had she just done?

***

Rick paced his way back to the cabin. He'd give her time. While he stomped his way back the argument started in his head between his common sense and the beast that had no goal other than mating. He didn't acknowledge the looks from the men on the porch. He simply walked past them. He went to his room where the air still held the heavy sent of their loving the night before. He paused to open a window, letting his body do things on auto-pilot. He packed his bag, put on clothes, tied his boots, and left the mussed bed behind.

The roar of his bike echoed off the hills and filled the vales of the Great Smoky Mountains. He hadn't spoken a word while anger chewed him up inside. He was bleeding and didn't know if it would ever stop. He hit a real road before Mitch's voice tore through his mental shield, cutting the argument he'd continued with himself.

Rick let the words flow through him. Manny would return to answer their questions, or not. He didn't know if he could care about this any longer. His heart was an open wound. The thought crossed his mind that he should have let the wound kill him. It would hurt less. He turned onto the highway and opened the throttle. Power shifted between his thighs and the wind offered sand-bitten caresses. He had no destination in mind.

***

Manny didn't know how long it took her to regain her senses. An hour, a minute, however long ago, Rick had left her without a word. Her Drakken wailed until Manny blocked her out. She'd gotten quite good at that over time. Manny stopped in the middle of dressing, her eyes wide with acknowledgement. She'd shut out the creature that shared her skin and mind so often that it was second nature.

"Drakken?" She plopped her ass on the fallen log, one boot in her hand, the other warming her foot, laces pooled on the ground. There was silence, deep and rich, as if she'd tossed the word into a chasm with no bottom. "Drakken." She added strength, but still the void between her ears kept silent. Manny finished slipping on her boot. On autopilot, she tied both sets of laces. Straightening her backbone, she lifted her shoulders back on a deep breath. "Drakken, you need to speak with me. Now is not the time to hide away." As if the Drakken had ever done so.

What is it that you want? There was no inflection in the reluctant voice, not one clue how the female interpreted the last scene between her and Rick.

"I want to apologize for shutting you out."

A little late.

"It is, but I didn't realize until now how much I relegate you to the back of my mind and ignore your council."

Don't think I haven't noticed.

"I would ask your council now."

It may well be too late. A heavy sigh accompanied the warning.

Manny heard the far-off buzz of a motorcycle roaring away. She couldn't blame Rick. He'd tried to be patient. He'd waited and then he'd pushed when he thought it was time. Manny hadn't given him the time, the energy, the concentration to connect with his needs or his wants.

You are guilty of that, the female in her body agreed. *He too is a proud warrior and you have spurned his every advance. He was willing to let you come to him, yet when you didn't follow through, when you turned him away, denied his claim, he left.* A whimper underscored her accusation.

Manny nodded and the roar of the bike faded until nothing surrounded her. In her world, this microcosm of self-doubt and confusion, the birds avoided the first note around her. She'd crushed the one good thing she could count on for her future. Now the rest of her life looked bleak and solitary. Manny stared into her heart. Had she allowed her past to sabotage her future?

I have no doubt you crushed your mate. He is a proud creature, one worthy of you. The sigh of the creature was so physical Manny shivered at the chill that enveloped her gray matter for a moment. *You will have to find him. There will be much to discuss between you, and even then, your prides must be put aside and common ground discovered.*

"Thank you, oh wise one." Manny kept the sarcasm from her voice as it flooded her. The result as it had always been, anger. She stood up and looked around the clearing. If she never saw it again it would be too soon. The leaves trembled with the force of her fury. Manny hadn't understood until then what the wind could do. With her emotions boiling like a sirocco in the desert, the leaves took the furnace heat from the air. Many of them curled in response. Immediately she blocked her anger off, leaving it tucked in a box with the other things she didn't want to examine.

Stepping over the log, she took a breath. If Rick had raced away on his bike, she doubted he'd shared their issues. The bedroom would be empty. She misjudged her next footstep and nearly went down. The hard step jarred her knee. She bit back the cry and kept moving. Her mind raced with solutions she discarded as soon as most appeared. He'd hide from her., keep away until he couldn't avoid her.

That's what she'd do. Hide, stay hidden. She'd been wrong to do so.

"Manny!" The call brought her focus back to her march. She hadn't decided if it was in shame or righteous anger. Lost in her thoughts, she was much closer to the cabin than she'd thought. Gareth raced across the mowed lawn toward her. "We have a problem."

"What's up?" She knew by his tone it wasn't about Rick.

"Laurel's been pinned down. We need a strike force headed out of here pronto!" Shoulder-to-shoulder they jogged back. Manny followed him in taking the steps in a long leap. In the living room Mitch had the others gathered and the rest of the team on speaker phone. She didn't hesitate but went up the steps and packed. Leaving her bag at the door, she stalked over to the bed and straightened the covers. It appeared as if the history made in the space had never happened. For now that was her only thought. It was the anchor that would help get her past this issue. Wondering if they'd called Rick back to duty, she grabbed her bag and headed downstairs.

"That's all we have." Mitch glanced up at her when she entered the room. He didn't give away any thoughts but greeted her with a short nod. "We are on our way out." He looked at Regina and Tracy, side by side at the kitchen door. "You want to stay here or come back to town?"

"I need—"

"BJ has—"

They spoke at the same time then glanced at each other. "We're coming back with you," Regina told him. Tracy nodded her agreement.

"Pack it up." Mitch shuffled the stack of papers in front of him as the room broke up in organized chaos.

Manny moved toward the door, ready to stash her things. Mitch stopped her with a grunt. She didn't turn to face him. Her hand tightened on her bag, but that was all the outward sign she showed of how little she wanted to do this with him right now.

"Rick tore out of here without a word. He was going out to

find you." Mitch stepped up to her. He studied her profile. He'd known she wouldn't give away any clue by even a twitch. "Know anything about that?"

Manny held her stoic expression by a thread. She straightened her spine, kicked her shoulders back, went to static attention. "I think I had something to do with that." An echo of her military training wanted to creep in and add the absent 'sir'.

"Is this something that will compromise you?"

"No, sir." She had no choice this time. He was questioning her ability to do her duty to the team and to the mission. She'd never allow anything to interfere with her laser focus on her job. The response snapped between her lips with military precision and curtness.

"Good enough." Mitch nodded and took a step back as Gareth entered the room.

That was as good as "Dismissed". Manny nearly ran out the door. She hoped he hadn't spotted the fine tremors that worked through her body. She was coming apart in slow progressions and she didn't know how to stop it.

CHAPTER 13

"Is she okay?" Gareth asked Mitch after he handed his bag to Mike to store in the vehicle.

"I don't think so." Mitch sighed. "Nothing is ever easy."

"Well, she's harder than most."

"No argument." Mitch took the bag from Regina and set it by the SUV door. "One last sweep of the place." The men made their rounds, securing all that the cabin encompassed. Mitch locked the door and then set the security system. Everyone else waited in the vehicles, seats taken and belts buckled. Mitch glanced at Gareth. Manny sat in the deep shadow of Gareth's back seat. He gave a small negative head movement.

Mitch inhaled silently. This would work out if he had to sequester them together for a month. He started the engine of his vehicle, heard the follow up of Gareth's and shifted into gear. They had a long night ahead of them.

***

Rick's eyes burned from staring at the sunset. He'd dropped south on a winding back road tour of Georgia. He'd hit the highway a few miles ago and joined the evening commuters into Atlanta. Now he searched for a hotel. Time to pull over for the night. His Drakken had been silent on the ride. Guess both had much to think about. The exit was coming up and he eased off the highway. The growl of the bike winding down exhausted him for some reason.

There was little sleep last night.

"I remember." Rick wished he didn't, but things along the road today reminded him often of Manny. Things like the curve in the road mimicked her shoulder or the curve of her waist. The outline of a mountain top, softened by time and the elements, reminded him of her breasts. Shadows crept from side to side as he navigated the twisting road southward, mental snapshots of her changeable eye color.

Now the setting sun brought to memory the wine color of her scales, the smooth underbelly of her Drakken in lighter shades. He was well and truly fucked. There would be no coming back from this if he couldn't make it work. He pulled into the first driveway and turned off the engine. The bike rolled onto the kickstand and Rick didn't move. He let the bike hold him as he paused. The sunset was behind the structure, night surrounded him, and he ached with a fierceness he knew neither alcohol nor exercise would banish.

He swung his leg over and took a moment to stretch. He thought of being hungry, thirsty, tired, but nothing made a lasting impression. He walked inside the motel, got his key, and went back to the bike. He'd been here before. If memory served, just down from the famous hotdog restaurant on the corner was a little pub. The food was unremarkable but filling and inexpensive, and the beer flowed into pitchers without pause. He hoped it was still there.

***

Laurel punched in the security code to his current residence. Both infants were doing well without their birth mothers. Sad thing that, women still dying in childbirth. He didn't give it another thought as he sipped the soda in his hand and opened the door.

The twins were watching over the children with help from the nurse he'd hired for that purpose. He took for granted he had the night off. There was a new paper he wanted to write. The information had been swirling around his mind all day, another jewel in his academic crown. These were the times he missed Yoseph Magellian the most. The aide would have the first draft of his paper done in hours. "Oh, well. Time to reacquaint yourself with the labor and research."

***

Mitch pulled up to their cabin and turned off the engine. They'd stopped outside the Atlanta city limits and taken four cabins on a one-night rental. Regina put her hand on Mitch's arm and tipped her head to Manny's solitary figure toting her bag to the cabin beside theirs. Manny didn't look back to see her team.

Gareth paused in following Mike, obviously watching his teammate, wishing he could help her.

"She won't open up. It's between them, Reggie." Mitch finished the ritual and left the SUV. They all had the power rides back. In a few hours they'd pile into one and head to the coordinates Jake forwarded.

The weight of their concern bowed Manny's shoulders. The burn of their gazes pricked her skin, even the thicker skin she donned as a defensive hide. Manny closed the door behind her and took her first full breath. Manny didn't know the last time she'd been able to do that. Perhaps when Rick left her alone. What she'd wanted, right?

The hours traveling and switching cars wore on her. Thankfully she rode with Gareth and Mike and they didn't seem to want to discuss much. She tossed her bag onto the bed and looked around. What she needed was a shower, a nap and to get her head solid. She did none of those things. She turned off the light and made sure the door locked. Then she moved into the bathroom filled a glass with water and drained it. The glow of the parking lot lights filled the windows and she made her way to the bed. Without pulling the covers back she crawled into the middle and piled the pillows under her head.

Forcing her eyes to close took time, and the fear she'd somehow connect through her relaxation to Rick on their mental pathway kept her from sleep. Thoughts swirled around in a dark carousel she couldn't pause or stop. The merry-go-round repetition did what nothing else accomplished. She fell asleep. Her shields weakened and her Drakken took over.

While Rick studied her, the Drakken studied his mate. She wouldn't relent enough to shower or undress. Her frenetic thoughts battered his weak defenses. He kept apart from her. It was a true learning experience. It didn't uncomplicate the relationship but gave him tools to work with. He wanted to go to her. The big orange bastard in his body wanted her. Rick hovered on the edge of her thoughts and watched, fighting the wanting inside him.

He didn't find anything in her mind about the impending mission. The half thoughts that he caught as she released them were of their fight this afternoon, the repercussions like waves curling before they crested, leaving him wondering what she really thought.

He drained the last mug of beer and stood up. Taking a couple of bills from his wallet, he stuffed them under the empty pitcher, grabbed his helmet and then he walked out of the pub. The night blessed him with a cool embrace. He stalked to his bike and mounted. The helmet muted city sounds and blocked his sight. The touch on his shoulder surprised him. He whipped the helmet off one handed, head slung back on his shoulders, spine snapped straight. One hand landed on his hip where his sidearm lived, fingers curled around the grip. The woman stepped back, raising her hand to her lips when she realized she'd startled him.

Senoia hadn't been thinking when she left the lab. She'd let her pace carry her through town and ended up here, turned about in the side streets of Atlanta. She was here on a scholarship and now interning with a renowned innovator in the realm of DNA studies. When she'd stopped wool-gathering she was here. And didn't have a clue where "here" was.

The big guy looked dangerous. His gaze had swept the streets and sidewalks before he mounted his bike. She'd thought to ask directions. When the helmet cleared his head, she gasped. He was rugged and handsome. His eyes narrowed when he looked at her a beat later, through her. Senoia shivered and everything feminine sat up and took notice.

"I'm so sorry." She reached out then stopped. He looked more dangerous now than he had moments ago.

"What is it?" Rick's voice dropped a note. He didn't see anyone but this woman around. Still, his nature and the alcohol soaking his instincts pressed forward. Defend, protect, attack filled him with energy and no outlet. He turned his gaze to look at the focus. A calm descended, no other way to describe it. The Drakken stirred, fighting the influence of her. It could be nothing else.

"Miss, is there a problem?" Rick's voice sounded gentle in his own ears.

"Um, no." Senoia dropped her gaze, her pale cheeks flushed pink in the neon glow from the pub. "It's just, well..." She glanced up and shrugged. "I seem to be lost."

Rick sighed, but his vigilance never eased. "Where are you going?" He propped the helmet on his thigh, kept his back to the wall of the pub. He remained hyper-aware of people passing behind him, across the empty street and at the intersection.

"I need to find Juniper. I have an apartment there." Senoia clamped her lips together. No need to babble her information to him, no matter how he tickled every erotic button.

"On the north-east side?" Rick brought his gaze back to her.

"Yes, I should be just a few blocks from it either way. The Varsity is over there." She pointed at the glow surrounding the next block, a corona effect of the neon lights that surrounded the popular eatery.

"You're off by two streets. Head down the block here, take a right." Rick jerked his thumb over his shoulder. "You'll see the sign." He two-handed the helmet again as she nodded and moved away. "Keep in the pedestrian traffic flow." He jerked the helmet down again.

Senoia didn't linger. Her footfalls faded quickly and Rick looked up to see her turn the corner and join others on the sidewalks of Atlanta. The interruption accomplished one thing. He'd stopped stalking Manny's thoughts. The connection, not very strong, was gone now. She'd probably fallen asleep. He cranked the bike, exactly what he needed to be doing. He pulled out and headed to his temporary room. Rick believed sleep would remain elusive.

***

Manny woke in the dark. She'd slept heavy and was nauseous and groggy. A glance at her watch told her everyone would be up and out shortly. She might as well get prepared. First she tied back her hair then braided the long strands to keep them out of her way as she worked. Her go-bag landed on the bed. She tugged the zippers and opened the compartments.

A mental inventory proved her always prepared for most anything. There was nothing in the bag Mitch would outlaw usage of if she needed it. She'd learned from him over the years. She glanced again at her watch. Time for a shower? She zipped the bag secure, checked the straps.

She took out her black BDUs like those all the operatives wore, piled them on top of the rezipped bag. In the small bathroom she stripped, turned on the water, waited while it heated up. Once steam gathered she stepped under the showerhead. Her hair she'd wrapped around her head and tucked in to keep it mostly dry.

A quick shower helped her mind tighten in focus and her body ease into morning. She dressed in uniform and slipped a knit cap over her hair. She repacked all her stuff and leaned it against the doorjamb. Ready to go, she stepped into the darkness of early morning. The Drakken stretched and examined the clues brought by the breeze.

No one here but teammates.

Manny smiled. The voice in her head was welcome. The Drakken had been silent for a long time. She knew it was because of the way she and Rick parted. The creature believed the humans would discover the correct course of action. All they needed was time. Manny wished she had half the confidence. Rick hadn't even looked back. She'd pushed him away once more, unable to confess to him what was happening in her mind. Maybe this time he was gone for good. Manny snorted as Gareth walked up.

"Manny, you packing?"

"You know it."

"Let's load up." Mitch moved silently to the truck they'd use. Gareth motioned for her to precede him and then took silent steps on her six.

Manny slipped into the back seat, setting the bag beside her. Her gaze lingered on the empty seat. Rick should be there. She'd run him off from duty. She fastened her belt and looked forward.

"Have either of you heard from Carlisle?" Mitch started the truck and leaned back against the seat. His gaze found Manny's in time to see her shake her head.

"Nothing. He's still sulking." Gareth waved at Mike, his lean partner headed back to bed to get up at a more reasonable hour. The trio would meet their families, if all went well, at home.

Mitch put the truck in gear as Gareth set the coordinates. The screen told them they were less than thirty minutes from their destination. Dr. Emerson Laurel had been careless and they'd found him again. This time he wouldn't get away from them.

CHAPTER 14

Rick startled awake, not sure what was wrong, only knowing that something was. He searched the room, glanced out the door. His bike sat unmolested where he'd parked it. He opened the door to his room and allowed his Drakken the freedom to use his senses.

There is nothing but our mate.

Rick started. "Manny's here?"

She is not here, she is near.

Rick closed the door. He ignored the snort and head shaking from his Drakken. He'd kept radio blackout too long. He grabbed his phone, ripped the cord off the bottom, and powered it up. He tapped the security code in and waited impatiently while the screen cleared. He had three missed calls, three voice mails and several texts.

One by one he opened them to find both Mitch and Gareth had tried to get a message through.

"We need you for the run at Laurel. Get back to me and I'll give you particulars." Mitch's voice was no nonsense. The same for the other call. "Look, Carlisle, we'll head out of here on mission at 0300. Get word to me."

That's why he snapped fully awake and alert. His team was bearding the lion without him. He tugged his BDUs out of his bag and dressed. The impatience of his Drakken dug into him, a weight on his shoulders.

"What is it?" Rick snapped to his other half. He'd sent two texts and neither Gareth nor Mitch had responded yet. He tossed the phone aside, poked his clothes into his bag and cleaned up the room.

She is not herself. The Drakken seemed to consider the words as he spoke them into Rick's mind.

"What do you mean?" The tone brought Rick to a complete stop.

She's not herself. There are gaps in her attention. She is thinking of the mission and of something else. The voice paused long enough for Rick to release a sub-vocal growl. *You have her distracted. Her Drakken will oversee her protection now*. The last comment was delivered in a dismissive tone. The lash of the truth stung Rick. He grunted as his anger lit.

"That might not be what Mitch needs her to accomplish."

That is the way it must be. She cannot walk into the operation with her mind split. She is dangerous to herself and others and not working at maximum efficiency.

Rick didn't know when the creature inhabiting him had learned so much. He strode to the phone, checking the screen for the last time. Letting it go dark, he slipped it into the cargo pocket of his uniform. "Can you track her down?" Reluctant to ask, he had no choice. Where she was, so was the team.

The Drakken snorted. Rick closed the door and dropped the kit into the saddlebag of his bike. Like it or not, he was joining them. He started the motor and waited for the biological GPS in his head to lead the way.

***

"Nothing?" Jake questioned.

"There is no office, no clinic, no computer. Nothing." Mitch repeated to his IT specialist.

"I followed..." Jake drifted off and Mitch heard the clatter of keys over the line. "Smart son of a bitch. I should have guessed. It means he has a tech on his side now."

"Any time, Jake. I'm listening." Mitch watched the empty building. Manny and Gareth were still searching for anything that might help.

"Boss, he's used the building to bounce the signal. I'm on the trace but you won't have the information for hours. I have to untangle all the leads and get back to you." Jake's voice lowered. "I should have looked for this, boss. I'll do better."

Mitch grunted and disconnected. The roar of a bike captured his attention as the noise ricocheted off the buildings around them.

Rick braked the forward track of the cycle and nodded to Mitch sitting in the SUV.

"Am I too late?" Rick pulled the helmet free of his head.

"Nothing to be late for." Mitch nodded at the doorway where Manny led the way out. "He's gotten smarter, according to Jake."

Rick hadn't heard him. He was busy holding the Drakken male back and eating up every stride, every mumbled aside Manny gave to Gareth. Jealousy choked him at their easy banter. He knew the team worked well together but... Still, Rick wanted to let the Drakken go, to give him control to take his mate and force her to understand her position in this screwed up relationship.

Yes, release your hold on me. The internal voice urged and Rick leaned away as Gareth stepped up.

"Not yet."

"You didn't miss anything, bro. Happy to see you." Gareth offered his hand and held it steady. He'd seen the change in Rick's eyes, noticed Manny not looking at him.

"You, too." Rick looked past him. "Manny, ride with me."

Manny stopped in the middle of her climb back into the SUV. She'd tossed her bag on the floor and one foot had landed beside it. One hand rested on the door and the other gripped the headrest to help pull her inside. Rick's tone of voice, the dominance, the command, broke through the false clarity she'd adopted. She looked over her shoulder at him.

He was a sight, that much she could admit. He lounged on the bike, one hand open on his thigh, the other gripped his helmet. His eyes caught the light and she loved the changeable color. The ginger stubble lining his cheeks and jaw made her hand fist. She wanted to touch him, let the roughness caress her hand, her belly, scrape the insides of her thighs.

"I didn't bring my helmet." Manny retained enough control to answer him. The female Drakken screeched in her brain, but she didn't flinch. Her chest ached as she watched him. His features dropped and those broad shoulders lifted in a sigh.

"I have an extra." He looked at her from under his eyebrows. The attitude dared her to resist. Hell, he wanted an open battle.

Manny took her leg out of the SUV. She hauled her backpack out with an angry tug and closed the door. Two steps took her to the window and she turned her attention to Mitch. In a voice nearly too low to hear she asked three questions. "Are you going home now?"

Mitch nodded once.

"Are we free to fly?"

Mitch glanced up through the windshield. Seeing the cloud cover and knowing dawn fast approached he shook his head. "Not now."

"You know how to reach me?" Manny wasn't sure if she felt relief or disappointment. With them effectively grounded the last battle wouldn't happen now, not that there wouldn't be a fight.

"You'll be with Carlisle?" Mitch asked his question as softly.

"Yes." The answer was a mere breath of sound.

"I want this straightened out."

Manny turned, tightening her lips. She gave a nod and offered her hand to Gareth. Gareth gripped her forearm, his fingers nearly meeting around her slender arm.

"Take care." He released her in time to hear the growl deep in Rick's throat.

Manny strode over to the bike and took the offered helmet. She buckled it down and adjusted her backpack. When Rick started the motor, she swung her leg over the seat and took her place behind him.

He didn't hesitate to pull out. She held him as he fed the powerful engine and they took the twists and turns away from the city. The highway beckoned and they headed north. Rick handled the bike as if they were two parts of a whole. Manny relaxed behind him. She hadn't slept much, just a battle nap, hard and deep, not nearly long enough. As the sky lightened to her right she let her head drop to his back.

She watched the sun rise, seeing cobalt blue give way to apricot, pink and then the rush of cornflower blue. Clouds started with shadowed bottoms then lightened to white cotton candy puffs. Her Drakken purred and there was the mental echo of another voice. The creatures were so in tune with each other.

"You want to stop a bit, stretch out?"

Rick's question broke the soft free flow of her thoughts. There was still so much between them. "Sure."

He pulled into the rest area at the border of Tennessee. Taking a spot away from family vacationers and business travelers, he parked. The lack of roar was loud for a few minutes.

Manny dismounted, took the helmet off her head, and rolled her head around her neck to stretch the tight muscles. She saw Rick reach for her from the side of her eye and stepped away as if she hadn't seen him. She secured the helmet and lifted her arms to do a full stretch. That woke her bladder.

"I'll meet you back here." She turned and started for the building. He was on her heels. She ducked into the women's side and let the door close before moving into the public area. "What the hell am I going to do?" Toilets flushed and the excited chatter of kids drove her into the closest stall.

You'll know.

Manny closed her eyes against the complacent voice in her head. She leaned against the door, knees weak as the creature swirled through her. Her flesh darkened in shade and every mental snapshot of her and Rick collided in her head. "Oh, no."

"Miss, is everything okay?" Manny glanced down to see the tip of a mop under the door.

"I'm fine. Thank you. I'll be out in a minute."

"No rush, dear." The mop and the concerned custodian left.

"Fuck it, fuck Rick, fuck you." Manny growled in a whisper. She flushed the toilet to cover the curses. She stepped out and glanced around. With no one in sight, she washed her hands and splashed her face with icy water. *No hot water taps on the sinks.* She stomped to the door and swung it open. There stood Rick, trying and failing to act nonchalant as he waited outside for her. "Thought I'd make a run for it?" Manny asked him, surprised herself at the belligerent tone of her voice.

"Not at all." He showed no surprise at her sudden attack. He held out a bottle of water to her. When she took it he finished his and tossed the bottle into the recycle bin. Long strides took him to the bike where he pulled his phone and scrolled through the information. An air of animosity clung between them, a sticky mass binding them together so they couldn't yet free themselves. Manny bit her lip then opened the bottle and emptied it. Hers joined his and she made her way back to him.

"I'm ready."

"Give me a minute." Rick finished the message. Mitch had given them permission to return to the cabin to work this out. They were both stuck from the mission until they could prove beyond a doubt their focus on the job.

CHAPTER 15

He pulled his helmet on, watching as she followed suit. He started the bike and pulled smoothly into traffic. He knew she'd be surprised at this turn of events. If Rick attacked, acted like a child? She'd raise hell and cuss and he'd have to snooze with one eye open. If it helped them to the conclusion of her overriding fear and his growing need to dominate her, he'd forego sleep. He remained puzzled by the turn of events, and he had to admit that her rejections hit him deep.

She tapped him on the shoulder when he missed the turnoff.

"We have permission to head to the cabin." He waited for her to explode. When nothing happened he glanced back. Manny didn't change her hold on him. Her body didn't stiffen with rage. She simply nodded and put her head down against him. His Drakken eased and accepted her weight.

They rode for the morning hours in the same positions. Occasionally she lifted her head and shifted her weight. He stopped for gas and bought lunch. They ate without speaking, standing beside the bike.

Rick followed the highway as far as possible. Then they moved onto secondary roads. The bike would have no trouble making it to the cabin, but they wouldn't have much to live on there. The staples would do, but they needed fresh food to go along with it. He pulled over about dinner time.

"We can stop ahead and get clothes and food."

"I can walk around a bit." Manny nodded, still tight within her head.

"Good." Rick noticed they kept the conversation light. When

dark fell the story would change. He expected the fireworks Manny surely stored to erupt in glorious light. He wanted so many things to happen. First he had to convince Manny to be his and not just her human side. Although, he thought as he started the bike, that side was most troublesome.

Too right. The lizard commented.

***

The dark silhouette of the cabin appeared as they made the last turn. Manny wanted to sigh in relief, but between the saddlebags being full and the extra in her backpack, there was no room between them to inhale. Her breasts rested against him, hell, they were flat against the planes of his back. Every twitch of his muscles massaged her nipples until she wanted to pinch them to points. She needed relief. Her pelvis snugged his ass and the leather seat heated things lower where she'd already dampened her BDUs. The rugged vibration of the motor kept her libido simmering and the enforced closeness took a toll on her. She'd never been readier to step off a bike.

Or take your mate. The Drakken spoke the truth so easily Manny wanted to nod. She couldn't though, because her chin tucked hard against Rick. She waited the next few minutes out. He kicked the stand back and dismounted. She slipped a bit then swung her leg over. He held out his hand to steady her. On her feet, she moved to the cabin with short steps at first then longer strides when the blood flow returned.

"Damn, double-damned seam." She tugged the crotch of her BDUs as she ascended the steps.

"Everything okay?" Rick's arms were full of the bags. He was closer to her than she'd thought.

"Yeah, good. I'll get the security system shut down." She took the last two steps in one and pressed her finger to the pad. The green light blinked and she lifted the cover to the keypad. After punching the numbers in, she waited for the light to go dark. The lock on the door clicked and the deadbolt slid back. She opened the door and took a stand to the side of the opening. Following her move, Rick took the other side.

Manny palmed her sidearm, crouched low and moved quickly inside the great room. Nothing had changed from night to night. Stale scents of food lingered, body wash added spice and the smell of charcoal made her long for a fire.

The last few miles in the dark had been chilly. The t-shirt under her uniform hadn't provided enough warmth, even with her clinging to Rick's broad back as a heat source. "All clear." He moved in behind her, his gaze roving about as he turned to the kitchen. No lights welcomed them. Manny closed the door before flicking the switch. Once that happened she knew Mitch got the notice on his phone. Couldn't keep anything from the boss. She shrugged out of her pack, relieved to put it on the floor.

She turned to follow Rick once she holstered her gun then changed her mind. The fire. She stacked kindling and a few bigger pieces of wood. Where the bag had rested against her sweat chilled her flesh. There was no way to be comfortable. "At least that seam no longer flirts with my clit."

"I never knew you talked to yourself."

Gods balls, he snuck up on me again. "Sometimes." Manny ran the long match against the rough surface to light it, smiling at the burst of flame. She held it a moment then moved it into the center of her careful pile. When the fire lit with instant crackles she dropped the match in to burn. She watched a moment, making sure before adding a real log. The greedy flames climbed the rough bark, a heated caress.

Mind out of the gutter. "There. We have fire, warmth, light." She rubbed her hands together and straightened. When she turned she saw Rick swallow right before he took her shoulders and kissed her.

He'd kissed her before, was it last night or the night before? She let the thought go. Those kisses were no class compared with this one. He didn't tease her into responding, he demanded her response. His lips pressed against hers and his tongue slid past her parted lips to claim her.

He cradled her head in one hand, the other pulled her into his body. His cock gave a kick against her belly and her hands rose to hold his shoulders. She thought to push him away, but the Drakken stopped the motion. Her hands curled, her palms roamed down his chest then back up. Manny thrust her hand through his hair. He kept it short, but due to business it had been a while since he'd seen the barber. She tightened her fingers on the curled strands.

He plundered her mouth, stealing not just her breath but the little sounds she uttered. A master devoured her. Her entire body heated, going up in flames like the conflagration at her back. He cupped her ass, fingers digging through the reinforced saddle sewn into the seat of her pants. She moaned aloud and he half lifted her to hold her closer.

Manny lifted one leg then the other and mounted his thighs. She couldn't believe this was happening. Not so quick. Sure, she'd known sex was going to happen. Good sex, hell, even great sex between them. The floating feeling engulfed her from oxygen starvation and lust sucked her under. Her back hit the river rocks that covered the front of the cabin's fireplace.

Good thing they were smooth sided. Rick paused to inhale then attacked her mouth again. Their tongues dueled and he won. The victor, he then turned his attention to her lips, sucking them into his mouth to play with. She startled when he bit her and nearly dislodged his hold on her mouth.

Her body melted. Cream pooled between her legs as things already needy cried out for relief. Her nails dug into his shoulders, his back, his scalp. Manny brought her hands together and pushed against his chest. Rick released her mouth and pulled away with a last bite to her chin.

"Too many clothes." Her voice came out thick with arousal.

"Right." Rick took her to the couch and sat down. His hands started on her shirt. He unfastened the buttons with broad motions. Every movement involved brushing his fists against her breasts.

She shuddered and closed her eyes. His taste flooded her taste buds, his scent clouded her thinking. Her eyes flew open again when he pushed the edges of her top apart and took her breasts in his hands.

"I've obsessed over these beauties." Rick cupped them from the sides and bunched them together. His thumbs flicked over her nipples, hard points getting harder from his deliberate attack. "I like your nipples tight. The color is so rich." He glanced up to see her face when he repeated the ping to her sensitive flesh.

The strain on her skin made her shiver with a lick of welcome pain. He kissed her captive nipples through the light cotton undershirt and the lacy cups of her bra. Not playing favorites, he showered attention on them both. Then he bedeviled her nipples with tugs before chewing them through the thin layers of fabric. She moaned and arched to give him more. He released her.

"Damn it, Rick." Her hand fisted in his hair and she tugged him back. He resisted and she opened her eyes.

"Hush, Pixie. I'm going to take real good care of you." He saw the long pupil, the black offset by the depth of the khaki iris. "Trust me?"

"Why ask?" Manny took a deep breath, shaken when his every word exhaled chilled air over her wet nipples. She shivered both from the unknown and what she knew to be true about her nature. His words dribbled over her in a slow drawl. The molasses accent filled her, delighted her, elicited the flare of desire and raised her lust astronomically.

"Trust me?" Rick didn't change the question. He waited for her response. Her hair loose from the half-assed wrap, she straddled his lap. Her braid looked good eight hours ago. Now he wanted to take it down. He did nothing but wait for her answer. Her uniform shirt bunched at her shoulders and the large wet circles left behind over her nipples begged his attention. Rick remained firm.

"You know I trust you."

"I know you'd fight by my side. You'd defend me to your death." He couldn't resist leaning in closer. "Do. You. Trust. Me."

His words filled her mouth and Manny closed her lips. The glow of the fire reflected in his gaze. The flicker brought gold and orange out of the hazel. His pupil split the iris, a sure sign his Drakken was close. She blinked. Of course she trusted him. Hell, had she led him to think she didn't? "I trust you, Rick." The mood temporarily cooled. She pushed on his chest to move off his lap. Settled beside him, she crossed her arms as she stared at the fire. "I'm not sure I'm trustworthy."

Rick took her hand and uncrossed her arms. "Help me with dinner and we'll talk it out." He didn't know the first thing about talking things out. Men discovered an issue, brought it up, fixed what needed fixing and cleared the air. There was no discussion. He stood up and hauled her to her feet. He kept her hand in his as he led the way into the kitchen.

Lights on, bags unpacked, they set to work.

CHAPTER 16

"So, about not trusting yourself." Rick sipped the wine he'd uncorked and poured for both of them. He stirred the marinara and watched the meatballs he'd mixed and put in the oven. The half-loaf of bread spread thickly with butter and garlic sat waiting its turn. On the other side of the sink Manny chopped veggies for the salad.

He watched her pause mid-chop. The knife she kept in one hand while the other hand mirrored his move. She lifted the glass and sipped with an appearance of calm. The clatter of the stem returning to the marble counter gave away her nerves. "There's a long history." She returned to the cucumber split on either side of the knife.

"I have nothing but time, and according to Mitch we are on leave until we straighten this out."

"He said that?"

Rick nodded, stirred the simmering sauce, and sipped his wine. He'd removed his uniform shirt and so had Manny, but the kitchen was warm. Her shirt had dried over her breasts. He missed the sight of her lacy bra cups. He gave her a few more seconds, watching her every move from the corner of his eye.

"So, I wasn't born a son." Manny took a deep breath and let it out slowly. She scooped up the chopped pepper and tossed it into the bowl with the other items.

"Thank all the gods and goddesses."

The drawl returned and her core heated up. Her Drakken wasn't immune to that hot southern charm. "Not like that." Manny retorted but couldn't hide the smile that flirted with her lips. He did make her smile, this rugged SEAL. "My father didn't have a son. So I took on the position. I did good most times. But later he resented that I didn't spontaneously grow a beard and a penis." She moved the bowl to the table then turned to face him. "He disowned me after my stint in the military." Her gaze glued to the wine in her glass, she reached for it and finished the last swallow. "He got to where he couldn't look at me without regret. I did everything, moved to the top in every class, every tourney." Her free hand waved with emphasis then dropped to her side, as discarded as she had been. She paused while Rick refilled her glass. "He died and I wasn't allowed to attend the funeral." She'd repeated these statements in her head often enough she delivered them in a conversational tone, like a speech she'd rehearsed so often the emotions it contained couldn't harm her. She sipped before continuing.

"Pixie, I'm so sorry."

"That's nothing, really. What hurt most was that to prove to him I was worthy of his respect and love *I* had to change. Those changes were difficult. I had to *be* the son. Then I had to be the young man. I proved time and again I was faster, stronger, smarter, better than the other guys because that way my father would love me." She sipped, savored, swallowed. Putting her glass down she looked up at him. Afraid now, she crossed her arms over her chest. She blocked the fear, held it deep inside.

"It didn't work. What it did was force me into a mental place where no woman should be." She moved to his side, kept his gaze locked with hers. "I have to be the fastest, strongest, smartest. To have me, you must do better than that. My fear is that I don't know the line I can't cross."

***

Rick swallowed past the dry spot in his throat. That little niggle that tried so hard to choke him when Manny delivered her concern. Rick tried to imagine any angle that caused her fears. He was prepared to deal with her doubts. She was so closed-mouthed about herself he'd imagined her worrying whether she was feminine enough. Perhaps she feared the Drakken. That was logical. Most of them started out fearing the uncontrollable beast. With work, they'd gotten past the fear and learned control. That was nothing compared to what she'd dropped on him.

He wasn't sure what to do, how to feel. Her body so close she nearly touched him from belly to groin, head tipped back, reality stared back at him from her eyes. How could any father do that to a wonderful daughter? The monster had molded her by rejection. He'd trained her by denying her love. He dismissed all that she was as a woman and then turned on her. After all, she was not his male offspring.

Rick couldn't laugh it off. Deeply disturbed about her status, Manny worried about besting him in a way to injure or kill. He wasn't stupid. Rick got that right off. Her greatest fear was losing control to the Drakken, mate to his lizard, keeper of his soul. She believed she'd best him in the mating plunge. Her trick of running away, of blocking off the growing relationship between them, of attacking when he got too close. For all of that he blamed the man who sired her.

"Rick?"

He didn't know how long they stood there. She was patient but not patient, and he had no clue what to say. Suddenly his mind spun through cause and effect. He needed to fix this, needed to assure her, but fuck him, he didn't know how. Not this time. "Um, yeah. That, there, uh..." He took her in his arms and held her gently. She didn't need another overbearing male in her life.

Yet to overcome the scars and damage of her early life, he was going to have to be just that. He inhaled her, inhaled the aromas of dinner. Scattered thoughts clogged his thinking. He didn't know what to say. Then a bell tinged somewhere and he smiled.

"Let's eat. Maybe we'll, it'll help—"

"Sounds good." Manny let him off the hook. She'd said all she could say on the matter. Obviously Rick had to internalize her struggle. She stepped back. The action pulled her away from the comfort she craved. She'd bared everything and the one man in her life now brushed off her concerns. Manny wasn't sure he understood. She turned to get the wine glass and picked up the bottle. Listening to it gurgle out the last of it, she nearly filled the glass to the rim.

Behind her Rick clattered dishes, opened and shut the oven, made domestic noises. She stared out the black window over the table. Her life as she lived it, endless blackness swallowing her until the only thing left behind was the expert, the soldier. Her eyes glazed and the glass surface focused, a mirror to her countenance. The girl she'd been blended into the woman reflected there. A hint of her Drakken peeked from those shadowed eyes and then was gone.

"Have a seat. I'll fill our plates. We have a long night ahead of us."

Manny startled and moved aside. "What kind of long night?"

Rick ignored her question. Her voice was suspicious and edgy. She'd confessed every dark secret. The one thing he and the big orange lizard agreed on? Get her into form and let her fly. From there he had no plans and the big lizard had no ideas. He dished out several meatballs and covered them with the marinara-coated noodles. The timer on the bread rang out. He put the pan on the stove, pulled on a mitt and used tongs to arrange two slices on her plate and two on his.

"Let's eat. I'll tell you what I think." He waited until she sat and then he took his chair. He watched her pick up her fork and drag the salad from the mixing bowl. She passed him the bowl and stabbed a forkful from her plate. Rick was grateful he had plan of action to get her past some of the issues she'd held onto for too long.

Damn straight. The lizard agreed with him.

"Shut up."

"I haven't said anything." Manny stared at him across the table.

"Damn, I said that out loud?" He put the bowl down between them then reached in and took a mandarin orange slice that gripped the side. Rick popped the sweet fruit into his mouth, as much to give him a moment to gather his thoughts as to quiet his Drakken.

"Sorry, it was the lizard." He swallowed. "Decided to put in his two cents." He dug into the spaghetti.

Manny took that as a signal he wasn't going to resume talking yet. She followed his example and started on her own dinner. After all the emotional ups and downs, at least her belly reminded her to eat.

***

"Okay. I think it's an appropriate time," Rick said. They'd finished dinner, had dessert, and finished another bottle of wine.

He'd led her to the porch and back into the swing. They'd talked of the mission, what seemed to lie ahead with the team, and exchanged a few 'when I was in...' stories of military life.

"For what?" Manny didn't dread what she thought was next. She wasn't looking forward to it, either. She'd been relaxed in the swing with his arm around her shoulders. They'd connected on several levels, finding common things in their experiences. She tensed at the sudden change.

"The fog has rolled into the valleys and the peaks are mostly hugged with mist. They don't call this the Great Smokey Mountains for nothing. Time to shift and fly."

"Oh no, Rick. I can't." Manny was on her feet again and moving down the steps when he caught her arm. Flight overran the fight instinct. She needed escape.

"You have to stop running away." He didn't yell it but kept his voice soft. This wasn't to be an arguable point between them. The Drakken agreed.

"I don't run." Manny snarled and jerked against his hold. She spun to face him. The rage on her features, lips tight against bared teeth, the lowered eyebrows, the light of her Drakken flickered in her eyes.

Rick stood his ground, his hand firmly around her forearm. He admired the muscle tone under his grasp. He kept it light but inescapable. "That seems to be your answer lately. We disagree and you disappear." He'd seen worse glares from his own reflection. She had nothing to scare him away.

Manny shook her head, paused as his words sank in, and stopped pulling against his hold. "You can give me back my arm." He released her. Manny didn't rub her arm. He hadn't hurt her. He'd let her come to her own conclusions. "You're right. I think this is important and I'm not sure I'm ready to deal with it."

"With what, Manuela? What particularly do you not want to explore?" Rick moved to the steps and slowly sank down. "We can take it one thing at a time. Whatever makes you comfortable." He clasped his hands between his knees and watched her reaction.

"Fears upon being a dragon 101." The words came easily, as easily as he switched from her given name, the shortened male version, and the nickname she hadn't decided she liked.

Rick would have laughed if any other teammate had uttered

those words in such a dramatic tone. This was his mate and she was serious. "Okay. Your first fear is?"

CHAPTER 17

Manny didn't answer right away. She looked everywhere but at him. Her mind grabbed and dismissed several openings. None were right. What could she say? "Shifting."

"Good place to start. Don't you remember doing it earlier?" Rick patted the step beside him. "Have a seat." Manny hovered on the edge of flight. He understood she didn't want to fight him, not yet. He wouldn't corner her, but he was going to help her integrate the two sides of her existence. He waited. He and the lizard were in perfect sync about that. The well-being of their mate took priority.

Manny reluctantly took the seat. She kept her gaze moving around the nightscape, avoiding a meet with his eyes. "I remember. There were other circumstances." Her voice drifted from the statement as if she didn't want to return.

"No worry, Manny. We made it through that. What I think would help you is to shift and fly. Use those wine-colored wings to drive your body high into the air. Find the currents that will hold you aloft. See the world from the pinnacle."

Manny heard it in his voice. He loved flying. The big orange Drakken that carried him aloft loved experiencing the night. Her Drakken rolled under her skin, a sinuous move that did two things. It made Manny aware she wanted to see everything for herself. The other was ignite the embers of desire into flames again. A yearning she hadn't thought she carried broke through. She could do this. Hell, she'd be the best once she learned how to control it. The immediate silence after the mental thought shook her. She carried her father around with her like an unbreakable locket, his training, his urging coming to surface at every challenge.

She'd had enough listening to him. Rick was right. It was time to see who she was without having to constantly prove her worth to a dead man. "Let's take to the skies." She got to her feet but wheeled on him before Rick go to his feet. "But just for flight."

Rick had been close enough for the big lizard to hear her thoughts. He knew what she was saying. His Drakken protested but silently and Rick nodded. "Just flying tonight. There are aerial maneuvers you should learn, but tonight is for fun."

Manny backed away and started unlacing her boots. Rick followed her lead. They dropped the BDUs and undershirts. "What do I do?" Manny wasn't self-conscious in the least.

"You are the most beautiful woman I've ever seen." Rick couldn't hold back the compliment. He didn't miss the flush of pink that warmed her skin.

"Mind on the mission, sailor." Manny scolded him, her bare foot tapped a quick tattoo in the pine straw laden yard. She'd crossed her arms. His compliment was sincere, both females wanted to preen. The Drakken accessed the feelings readily, Manny was not so open.

"Gotcha. Let the Drakken talk to you. She knows now how to move between forms. Bypass the kin. We'll get into combat with that one later." He took a few steps back from her to give her room.

Manny remembered the incredible sex they'd shared in the kin form. What would it be like to fight in that form? The strength was infinite. The pleasure doubled.

Mind on the shift or you'll land on your ass.

That was all the warning the Drakken gave her before shifting them to the winged form. Manny didn't have time to register any pain. Her mind believed there had to be some.

There is, I'm simply hiding it from you. No need to experience that in case you need to shift and respond to events around you. With that reassurance, she gave a little jump and engaged her wings. This time the detritus swirled around her by her actions instead of her thoughts. The chill of night embraced her as she swept into the skies. The taste of the fog delighted her. She snapped at the billowing mist. The haze parted for her sharp snout but left behind droplets that collected into tears on her angular face. The wetness she welcomed, letting it coat her eyes. She snorted it out of wide nostrils. Flying into an open space, she glanced around. The fog fitfully occluded the moon, allowing it to peek out in short rare bursts.

Over her shoulder, his wings lighter in the night Rick kept pace with her. She dropped altitude and lashed her tail on a last-minute turn. He kept up with her. She turned vertical, pushing her wings to take her high, then higher still. The fog disappeared behind her, and the moon in a perfect crescent greeted her with a lopsided smile.

The air chilled, grew colder against her scales. It was thinner and Manny had to work harder to grip the friction to boost her higher. She fought for every yard until there wasn't enough air to lift her. She couldn't breathe and the threat of passing out clouded her sight for a moment.

That's enough.

The whip of Rick's mental shout made her smile. He was below her, and worried, and watching her float in the rarified atmosphere that had little to no oxygen. She released the hold she had, letting her wings spread wide to keep her descent slower than a dive. One last look at stars so crystal the light hurt her eyes and she let gravity pull her down.

The air thickened and her breathing returned to normal. Rick joined her, his body much closer now. She drew in deep draughts, fueling her wings with energy. They circled peaks both treed and barren granite. A small herd of deer played in the moonlight before bedding down for the night. Manny buzzed the little community, scattering them to the woods.

The flight lifted her spirits. The fragmentary seam that existed between her and the Drakken fused. They came together with mutual understanding. She looked for Rick again, her great orange shadow. She remembered flying over a flat-topped peak and wanted to pause there. Of one mind, the females had a plan. Pivoting in midair, she backtracked to the place she chose. The wind off her wings whistled at her speed. Rick kept pace right behind her. She circled the peak, checking for signs of other habitants. Not that they wouldn't run as soon as two Drakkens landed. Certain it was clear, she tucked her wings and dived to the surface.

Manny, slow down!

The strong mental shout made her laugh. She knew exactly what she was doing. The ground rushed up to greet her, shades of unforgiving grey. One miscalculation on her part, if her Drakken's knowledge of physics was incomplete, and her blood would coat those rocks on landing. The boulders grew larger and something inside of her struggled to avoid them.

You have the understanding. The encouragement from the wild half of her assured Manny and she extended her wings fully, battering the wind to brake her momentum. As soon as she knew weightlessness, the loss of gravity, the complete halt of forward movement, she furled them and shifted to her human form. Manny remained on bent knee while Rick settled and then shifted back. The smirk might never leave her face. He and the big lizard sputtered at her as he approached.

"You can't test the limits of your flight velocity like that." Rick stomped up to where she knelt on the granite slab. "If you'd miscalculated by one aeronautical knot of speed you'd be a thin red smear." He gestured widely with his arms, flinging them about as he scolded, lectured. He stalked around her, and Manny wisely kept low to the ground.

"You took a decade off my life, damn it. I won't have you *pushing* the envelope before you know the dimensions of the envelope." He stopped in front of her. She hadn't made a sound. Goddess damn, what if she'd gotten injured? He went to his knees and reached for her, only to hesitate at the last minute.

"Fuck stick." Manny lifted her head. Her face reflected her mirth.

Rick paused before he grabbed her. He'd meant to shake the shit out of her. Instead he studied her features. Filling her eyes, along with the mirth, was confidence, pride, the exultation of her first flight. Her cheeks carried the fresh kiss of their night flight through clouds of fog and mist. He couldn't be the bastard who called her down for any of that. Let Mitch be the bad guy. He didn't have time to brace before she launched herself into his arms.

"Oh, Rick, it was magnificent. I was flying and the air was thin and the stars so bright."

Rick held her on top of his body. He'd take care of the scratches along his back and ass after his next shift. She weighed nothing buoyed by her excitement. He wanted to capture this moment in a bottle. Instead, he memorized this time forever committing it to his gray matter. This was what he'd known existed within her. If he was patient, if he respected her enough to listen, to hear what she said, if he gained her trust and love, *this* was the woman who waited for him to unlock things she kept inside.

"You were beautiful." He made the admission when she wound down and stopped squirming atop him.

"So were you. Your Drakken is huge."

"Not as large as Mitch's is. You'll see him soon. We'll practice together." He kissed the tip of her nose.

Manny blinked at the kiss. Only then did she realize she was nude. They hadn't brought clothes, of course. They'd left them folded on the porch at the cabin. The Drakken didn't mind her position at all. Rick's cock rose in that tick of silence. The hot column nestled between her pussy lips. "I'm not the only one excited." The whisper enclosed them in a bubble of intimacy.

"No." Rick wondered what she was thinking. They'd been here before. Of course there'd been a lovely soft bed under them.

"I don't want to change anything between us." Manny settled her weight, still for the first time since she'd launched herself at him.

"This happened before and nothing changed."

"It did. You walked away." Manny's face lost all animation.

CHAPTER 18

Rick hadn't known what that would mean to her. The transparency was evident. All that she'd disclosed earlier skipped through his mind. Highlights of the way her mind worked, the parts that formed the essentials of the woman he was fast falling in love with. That was the logical part of his mind. The physical remained focused on the heat and wetness coating his cock. "I didn't know then. I know now." He took her head in his hands and brought her lips to his.

She could kiss him endlessly. He took her in a storm of passion, every flick of his tongue like lightening along her nerves. She tasted the garlic, the tomato sauce, and the essence that was Rick. She danced her tongue through his lips, taking and letting the sensations stack until she couldn't resist pumping her hips. His cock slipped over nerves that sparked deep inside her empty channel. She wanted him harder and closer. The goad between her thighs, his dick tapped against her, the slickness he brought from her, the dew of her excitement slicked the length of him.

There were no condoms here. The same time she thought it he broke the kiss. "Condoms."

"Right." She licked his flavor off her lips and pushed upright. Both moaned. "I can't get pregnant."

"You mean now is not the time." Rick hoped that's what she meant. In time he wanted a child or two. She'd been in positions, some of them potentially fatal. He'd seen her body and there were several scars he'd like to ask about.

"Right. Not now."

"Turn around." Rick's intonation dropped and the Drakken

joined him in the short order.

"What?" Manny blinked at him genuinely confused.

"Turn your body around. I want to taste you."

"Oh." The picture cleared. She switched her position. Now she faced the hard length of him. He grasped her hips and tugged her until satisfied with her position. She drew in a breath when she felt him part her swollen lips to find the creamy center. Not finished, his tongue swiped lower to catch her clit. The electric jolt nearly unseated her. His hands tightened to hold her and didn't let go.

She could do this. She took him in hand, seeing the glisten of her natural response along the length. Sticking out her tongue she licked him, happy when his stomach sucked in under her. Another long lick, she took more of her taste into her mouth. His groan vibrated against her clit and she moaned in return. Unable to wait longer she opened wide and slipped his length past her lips and into her mouth.

She stopped when the threat of gagging hit her, backing him out just a bit. She attacked the inches she held in her mouth, using suction and a tongue lashing, which he returned. This was turning out to be a contest. He was going to lose. Manny pulled him from her tight lips and blew air across the damp flared head. She watched it expand then exhaled to warm her mouth before taking him deep again.

She cupped his balls. The thin skin didn't offer much protection. The balls inside the sac filled her hand and she treated them gently. Holding them in her palm, she cupped and rolled them in the wrinkled flesh.

Her lips and tongue worked his cock, her gentle hold of his nuts had him stretched on a rack of pleasure. Rick forgot to breathe. He blinked when she tugged, creating a bit of *unpleasure*. The ragged sensation cooled his passion, backed him away from the flashpoint of orgasm. He went back to work on devouring her. She'd just notified him he was going first. A contest of sorts. If that's what she wanted, he'd play. When they got back to the cabin he'd show her the winner.

He parted her delicate inner lips, applying tension enough to get her attention. It worked. Her head lifted from him, and a tight moan slipped from her throat. He delved two fingers into the portal in front of his nose and followed her example by closing his lips on the nexus of her pleasure center. With a twist of his wrist he smiled when she bucked. He'd found her g-spot. He was about to blow the top of her head off.

Manny returned to her task, the pleasure and power intermingled. He'd reminded her of her feminine core by the hard stretch. She was so close her skin dewed, so close tears filled her eyes. The orgasm she wanted, needed, craved, hovered just out of reach. She took him deep in her mouth, deeper than before. Holding her breath, she rocked her mouth down his shaft. The flared crown entered her throat and she held him there while she worked her tongue on the flat surface.

No air passed the thickness of him filling her throat. She held him tight until the threat of passing out darkened the edge of her consciousness. She pulled him back, releasing him slowly and teasing every centimeter with the continued suction and the flick of her tongue. The taste of his precum lingered in her throat and chills worked over her when he slowly teased the walls of her vagina. "I'm close." She couldn't stop the words. In her hand, another sweet pearl formed and she lowered her head to take it as her due.

His cock slippery from being in her mouth, she worked her fist from the base to her lips while her tongue danced over the crest. She wanted more of his flavor, rich sea salt and sweet corn. Manny held him hard, twisting her fist now as she worked. Rick hit the right combination and she hummed her appreciation, curling her hips to get closer to every lick, every thrust of his fingers. He'd added one to pair and stretched her wide as deep as he could reach.

Rick's balls tightened as the vibration of her hum traveled through her lips and down the shaft to his sac. The impulse left his dick behind, rocketed up his spine to detonate in his brain. She wasn't the only one close. He needed to hurry her along before he shot his load. Damn, did she like the taste of a man? He disconnected from her and licked his lips. Her hum of disappointment nearly undid him. "I'm close, Pixie."

"Ye-ammm." Manny nodded and hummed and swallowed his cock until the pinch of her throat released his orgasm.

He dug his heels into the rock under him, unable to stop the thrust of his hips to her talented mouth. Jets pulsed out his dick until his toes curled, the raging release calmed to flutters. She'd taken every drop. He knew she'd swallowed the first loads down. Holding his spent cock in her mouth she gently worked her way around the crown, taking every drop without overloading his senses from pleasure to pain.

They were both going to be winners. As soon as some semblance of normal returned to his heart beats, he pulled her back to his lips. Wrapping them around the nub still urgently distended from the protective hood, he suckled. Her body stiffened at the erotic caress. He kept the tension in her body as he slipped two fingers back into the wellspring of the cream that coated his lips, his chin, his nose. Hell, he knew his cheeks were wet and slick. She tasted of brine and sin and he'd never get his fill.

He thrust deep then turned his wrist to drag the tips of his fingers over her g-spot. She shuddered and her grip fisted tight around his half-hard cock. He was doing all the right things. He repeated the move three more times before she tossed back her head and screamed her release. He sputtered when she came, the flavorless effusion running down his cheeks.

Like he had done, she pumped her hips down to him, the ancient movement designed to pull him deeper inside. He thrust three fingers inside and the muscles in her vagina pumped against his fingers in tight convulsions he wanted to feel against his cock. He flattened his tongue and placed it against her clit. The moan rose to a shout and she bucked away from him, dislodging his fingers. Manny collapsed on top of him ambushed by another wave of orgasms.

The shudders eased and stopped. Rick rubbed her back and the back of her thighs as she recuperated. He sat up. He moved her leg over his chest and tugged her arm to get her to move.

"I'm dead. You just killed me."

"You're not. But we're on heat-sucking rock. I get that you want to rest. I want you up here." He smiled and waited while she got to her hands and knees and followed his directions.

"Sorry 'bout the dribble," she mumbled, her head on his shoulder, her body lax over his.

"You constantly amaze me. I didn't think I could lose more than my heart and soul." He drew lazy circles on her back with one hand and held her hand in his other. "Ever wonder how many women would like to do that? How eloquently your body tells your partner he's amazing? He's taken you beyond an orgasm. It's potent, makes me feel like beating my fists and yodeling." He took a breath as if to try. Her hand rushed to cover his lips. He chuckled. "Pixie, I'm the man." He took the tail of her braid in his fist and tugged her face up to his. Kissing her, he rolled them until she lay cradled in his arms.

He looked into her eyes after breaking the lip-lock. "We need to head back."

"A nap?"

"In the bed at the cabin." Rick pushed up to a plank then walked his hands down beside her. He got to his feet and held out a hand. "Come along, mate. Let's go home."

Manny watched him. For the first time in quite a while she experienced exhaustion on every level. Her mind drifted in its own fog. Her body felt like mush. Her thoughts moved so slowly that some perished in the process. She watched him curl his fingers in a 'come on' movement. Did she love him?

You do, with body and soul. Now get your ass up and let me drive. The Drakken didn't mince words.

Manny took his hand and swayed a moment as the blood settled back into proper currents. Steady, she nodded and released his hand. Rick stepped back and Manny let the Drakken take control. On four feet, wings opened at her side, she wanted to trumpet success, her newly discovered ability for love, the strength of her femininity. Regina had been correct. She needed to let the world know her happiness.

"Not right now." Beside her, a gust of wind introduced Rick's big Drakken. "Head out. You remember the way." He moved back a few more steps to give her room. He watched as she gathered her wings and raised her head. If he'd known what she'd do next he'd have tackled her and given her a less enjoyable tongue lashing. Instead, he sucked in a panicked breath and watched her catch the current under her wings. Heart beating way too fast, he loped the few steps to the edge, his feet already leaving the rocks as his wings worked to lift his body. She needed a spanking for scaring him.

I don't think she'd allow that, knowing what we have uncovered about her nature.

You're right. Rick dipped a wing and followed the curve. He enjoyed the simple freedom. The night had blessed them early with fog and Manny took to the air as if born there. In a way, she was. If her outburst in the clearing earlier was anything to go by, Wind Dancer should be her Drakken name. Clearly the air responded to her.

He kept her in sight all the way back to the cabin. She did the same move to land and while every muscle seized up from head to tail, Rick admired her control. She knew the instant her wind speed dropped to fold her wings and start the shift in form. She kept her pose, one knee and hand balanced on the ground, head down.

CHAPTER 19

He circled the area, the Drakken scouting for anything out of place, a last round by the guard before bedding down. Rick didn't hurry the process. Keeping Manny safe was a primitive biological necessity. When the circle diameter included the cabin and two miles around, he took the direct route to the cabin.

Manny swung on the porch, dressed except for bare feet, water bottle in hand when Rick landed. She watched him regain his balance and walk toward her. She'd known what he was doing and for once didn't bristle at the notion he had to 'look after' her. In a way it was nice, gave her a warm fuzzy feeling she'd never had before.

She'd had time to ponder things, '*think on 'em*' as one of her staff sergeants used to say. Rick now knew the secrets in her chaotic mental closet. He'd seen the damage. She didn't know what he thought about her state of mind. She was also dealing with her shift and flight and the mind-blowing orgasms she'd had on the rock. She sipped the water, pushing the swing into motion, watching him cross the yard and come up the steps.

"I thought you'd be inside." He took the offered bottle from her hand, twisted off the top and drained it.

Manny's gaze stalled on the actions of his throat, the strong column of his neck. From there she contemplated his wide shoulders. She'd never thought about the male body. Hell, she was so innocent in that regard. She'd been on the other side with her mates for too long. That mind set she learned long ago. She'd served beside men like Rick all her career. After getting out of the service she'd joined EOD in several cities while she'd moved around looking for a home. Most explosive ordinance disposal officers didn't last long. The stress of disarming and transport took its toll on the nerves. The job was as diverse as the military in the same field, which meant there were very few women in bomb disposal.

Returning to her study of Rick, Manny considered that she had never once "seen" one of her teammates. They were skeletons with muscles and attitudes and intelligence. She depended on them and them on her. Looking at Rick was like a strange dissection of one of those teammates. Most were male. She believed it was the field. Rick stood fast in the face of incredible transformation. He'd had to make the adjustment alone to sharing his skin with another intelligent being, one who possessed the single-handed ability to wipe out a tank, or with his size, a small naval vessel.

The plastic bottle crumpled in his fist and startled her out of her musing.

"I think it's time to head inside." Rick picked up his pile of clothes and waved his hand for her to precede him.

Manny got to her feet and led the way inside. The fire burned low. The warmth that filled the room was soft, inviting. She dropped her boots inside the door and crossed to the wood bin to add several more logs. The night was cooling off and they'd want the warmth come morning. Hungry flames sucked the new fuel and the room brightened. Manny turned to see Rick pulling drawstring pants over his hips. After one tug of the string he looked up to meet her gaze. "You are awfully quiet."

"I've been thinking." Manny curled her leg under her before she took a spot on the sofa.

"I may need more than water for this discussion." He made the retort light but couldn't explain why his chest tightened.

"I'll take a glass." Manny focused on the fire, relaxed more than tired. She heard the soft approach of his bare feet.

"Here you go." The red wine sloshed up the sides as he poured. The darkness glowed with the orange fire behind it. She sipped and smiled as he continued around the sofa and sat down.

"Thank you." Manny held her glass out. Rick tipped his until the sides tapped.

"I think I'm ready." He half turned to look at her. The bottle rested beside his foot. He took a deep breath and then a hefty draw on the wine.

"You know what you're up against." Manny lifted a shoulder. She sipped, let the crackle of fire eat the wood to fill the silence.

"It's not so much, Pixie."

Manny wasn't sure she like the tacked-on endearment. It was loads better than that idiot Trevor calling her *Pigpen*. Still, it was a nickname. She'd avoided them her entire life, quashing every title in her career. There was something about the way Rick said it, though. His tone softened, became intimate with the word. She decided she liked it, only from Rick. Only in private moments like this.

"We all have things we need to work out. You should know, since you came *Below* to rescue all of us. We have issues, scars, things that bring us upright in the middle of the night. We pace, we fret and we aren't the best at sharing." He took her free hand and wove his fingers through hers. He pulled tight, bringing their palms together. "Baggage." He met her stare. "Look, I know it seems a lot for you. Why do you think the Drakkens would recognize a mate if it wasn't a real match?"

Manny hadn't turned the situation on its side before. "I don't know. It shouldn't happen. Natural selection would dictate only the most compatible would be able to mate."

"That is what our Drakken have been trying to tell us all along."

"Rick, you were made a Drakken by chemical alteration of your DNA."

"Pixie, you were made a Drakken by the biological alteration of your DNA."

"That's not what I'm saying. You bought into this as enlisted. I didn't have a choice. By the time we figured this out, I was already infected." She held up their clasped hands. "Not saying the infection is a terrible thing. I'm fortunate to have time to adjust. I didn't experience the horror you lived through, all of you. What I'm trying to say, I guess, is that I carried my past into this situation without understanding how it would turn out in the end."

"Honey, Pixie, we aren't at the end of this."

"And that fact, Rick, is why I'm not ready to face this." Manny disconnected their hands and got to her feet.

Rick watched her pace. Manny glided over the floor, her bare feet long and lean. The nails were unpolished. She was definitely a no-nonsense kind of woman.

"What is it you're so afraid of?" Rick fought back the frustration. He didn't know how many more times he could ask the same question.

Manny glanced at him from the fall of her hair. After she'd shifted the braid was history. She hadn't bothered to tie the long fall up. He loved it, the peek at her from the platinum strands aroused him. "Fuck, everything about you arouses me."

"What?"

"Nothing. I didn't mean to say that out loud." Rick followed her to the fireplace. He paused to put his wine glass on the mantle. "Look, I'm stronger than you think. Your Drakken knows this. I bet she's been whispering encouragement to you and you've just shut her down. Like you've tried to shut me down." He took her shoulders, so fragile and so strong, in his hands. She locked her gaze with his and he could see the contradiction form on her lips, in her eyes.

"Not only are we Drakken mates, Manuela, I love you."

Manny didn't twitch. He'd certainly put everything out there. What if she'd lost him before the Drakken guardians had intervened to heal him? What if he'd died before her Drakken had him to recognize, to hunger to possess? What if...

"I can't promise I won't kill you, Rick." The tortured whisper escaped. Her hands clenched and only then did she realize she'd lifted them to his waist.

"Then let's get back in the air. We'll see what happens. Because I can't keep playing this 'what if' game with you, Pixie. I'm tired of getting close only for you to push me away. This is right and I can show you that your fears are groundless." He gave her a shake and lifted his gaze from hers to glance out the window.

"We don't need much time and the night is young. We have hours yet to see." He kissed her forehead then rested his head against hers in that exact spot. "Come with me, let's take this dive." Rick didn't coax her further. He'd felt the full body shudder as her fear wanted to take control again. She'd agree or he'd have to leave Mitch's service. It boiled down to all or nothing for Rick. He wasn't going to force her to have him. She had to come to him of her free will, she needed to overcome the crippling fear she carried of killing him.

Rick had no such fear. He was her male mate, her dominant, her superior. No matter her training, her thoughts, or her fears. She belonged to him, and as soon as he made his claim, took her for the mating dive and made her his beyond any doubt, she'd know. Manny would recognize they were partners and lovers and stronger together.

"Okay."

The one word slammed into Rick so hard it took his breath. He didn't hesitate. He turned her to the couch. "Get them off." He followed his own order, dropped the pjs in a pile and stepped out of them.

He opened the door. He and the Drakken judged the time. "We have at most three hours. She'll fight tooth and nail. Should I have the Doc on standby?"

We heal when we shift. We heal with time. The Drakken paused. *When she becomes ours, love will heal the worst*. Rick nodded and twisted to look at her when her hand touched his back.

"Now or never." Manny nodded at him.

Rick closed the door behind them, took her hand and led them off the porch. He shifted first and took to the skies without a backward glance. He was heart-sore from her rejection, and part of him, a little part he kept shouting down, expected her to deliver the final blow.

Wing beats joined his and his emotions swung again. He made two turns around her as she steadily winged her way to more isolated stretches of mountain peaks. He took a spot just behind and to the right of her.

With the granite table under them, Manny chose that moment to climb. The sight where they'd made love was a beacon and gave her courage. She flew vertically until the air chilled and grew thin. At her side, Rick pumped with power and grace and kept pace. Her Drakken screeched, a shrill cry of need the instant before she turned on the male beside her. Her attack was a shock to Manny, but the Drakken didn't hesitate.

Rick paused between wing thrusts, a hover of sorts while he watched Manny. He knew she'd made up her mind. The female dove at him, her neck stretched and her teeth bared. She used her wings as both stabilizers and steering. He admired her a second too long and those teeth scraped his shoulder before he twisted away.

CHAPTER 20

Damn it, if he'd hung there longer she'd have gotten his wing. He'd be in sorry shape. The attack told him all he needed about her intentions. He fell through the night, only to use the greater speed to loop around her. Folding his wings in he dropped to her back. Rick caught her with his legs and together they plummeted toward the earth.

Manny stiffened then relaxed. When Rick eased his grip, she turned to her side and broke out of his hold. Wings spread, she stopped the fall and started to spiral upward. Keeping him in her sight, she turned as he headed up to her.

The wild nature of the Drakken was her guide, the hard lessons her strength. Manny dove at him, this time her arms out, claws ready to rend and tear.

Rick couldn't avoid this attack. He could only admire her until they met. Her weight slammed into him, taking him down. The claws burned where she dug in. She wasn't at all playing at this. He bit her shoulder where her wing joined her body, breaking the scaled flesh, and tasting blood.

She squealed and released him. Rick didn't turn her loose. He let momentum carry her under him then clasped her close to his body. With her wings hampered, she couldn't beat her way free. He carried them up beyond her flight path. He was both bigger and stronger in Drakken form, with a wider wing span. When he gasped for oxygen he released her. She'd stopped struggling moments ago. He turned and watched her fall. She tumbled with no grace. He tucked his wings, feeling the sting of her wounds. He dove after her, caught her, and halted them. His wings grabbed thicker air.

She trembled in his hold, her bright eyes focused on him. Rick turned them belly to belly, adjusting their greater form. Manny curled her neck around his and he waited for her bite. When those six-inch teeth didn't strike him, he thrust deep into her pussy. Her roar filled the night and she pushed free of his hold. Rick growled back at her, a deep purr of reprimand. He caught her again, hauling her body back toward the stars, cloaked in fog.

The minute they paused in the upward flight, he clasped her to him and again found the slick entrance to her body and staked his claim. He snaked his neck around hers. Her teeth were dangerous. They fell through puffs of mist. Rick's hips ground against Manny, thrusting deep then deeper still with a slight adjustment.

The fall, the mist, the feel of her cunt enclosing his dick took his breath. The night was perfect and he kept pumping until lightning filled his sight. He released her, slipped from her body, and caught the updraft with spread wings. His body wasn't nearly done with the claiming.

Manny flipped, opened the webs that allowed her flight and stroked away from him. She still savored his blood in her mouth, the slickness of her pussy a reminder how good their coupling felt. She had to think, but the Drakken wanted more of him. The animal controlled her now, and what she wanted, while a match to Manny's desire, she experienced differently.

Manny sighted Rick. The Drakken began an aerial dance -- loops and twirls to show off her prowess at flight. She preened and crooned at Rick. She demanded he accord her attention. A not so subtle demand. She ignored the pain in her wing but favored the injury as she sky-danced for him. The lure worked and the male drifted closer to her. Manny snorted, little head hard, big head soft. One more down stroke and he'd be within striking distance. She needed to ground him, to dominate the skies.

Her spell wove around Rick so tightly he couldn't help but fall under her bewitchment. There was no need to resist her. He and the scaled creature wanted her again and once more before the sun rose. After that Rick wanted her. The mating hadn't claimed them yet. They had more time to play. He'd barely finished the split second of thought before she attacked. The mid-air broadside that took him by surprise.

Determined, Manny drove into his body. She bowed, using her back legs to rake claws across his belly. The softer flesh tore. The scent of blood joined the scent of pheromones in the air and she pulled away, stroking higher as quickly as her wings could carry her. She watched for a counter attack. It wasn't long in coming.

Rick didn't glance at the stomach wound. For the second time in just days she'd tried to gut him. The blood and sex called to him with mind-numbing passion. The instinct he'd blocked from his wild side he now released. It was time for them to claim her, to put the ridiculous fears she harbored to rest once and for all. The time for being nice was long over.

He shook the primal stimulant mix of scents from his head. Above him she'd taken another stance. He stroked up, this time going straight to his prize. She hesitated, watching to see if he would veer off. She waited too late and he was on her. He'd have to tell her about playing "chicken" as a teen. He'd never lost his nerve.

Taking her throat under her jaw in his mouth, Rick dragged her up as his wings kept his trajectory. She had to stroke alongside of him or risk his tearing her head off. He didn't care. Even with her wings operational she couldn't attack. He led her up until the air thinned again, the trickle of her blood into his mouth a potent aphrodisiac with the lust steadily fueling his energy. He turned her without issue, clasped her body to his and drove his dick deep. Her body accepted him, even though she'd absorbed his earlier release.

He pressed deep and tightened his hold. Rick folded his wings around hers and let gravity have them. Hips pumping, viciously stretching her tight channel to accept everything, he took her blood and set his claim.

Manny trilled through her throat. The Drakken keened inside their shared mind. The creature accepted the claim and yet Manny fought. She struggled to free herself, but the first wash of his ejaculate warmed her inside. The hot jets splashed against slick walls. The burst of healing surprised her by easing the pain of his stretch.

She moaned, the sound close to the same from both human and Drakken throat. Rick released her neck and she curled her neck around him to take another grip on him. Her teeth just pressed through the scales to reach his blood, taking the sip to seal the claim. At her human's acceptance, the Drakken arched her back and offered her body up to the wild hunger. Fire bloomed through Manny and she let Rick hold her, taking them up again for another dive. The carnal embrace tore through mind and body and Manny gave herself up on the altar of consent and submission.

Rick took them skyward three more times. The last time she shivered in his hold, her passion exhausted. He let the false dawn embrace them, the fog and mists made thicker by the heat condensing off their bodies every trip. A blast of heat moved through him as he attained the summit for the last dive, his body remained lodged inside of the sweet heat of her pussy.

They hesitated before the drop. *I love you, Manuela Cox.*

I love you, Richard Carlisle.

Rick's cock grew, pushing against surfaces already stretched to accommodate the Drakken's size. Nodules caused pain that increased when the nodules became spikes. Rick couldn't hold them motionless and Manny writhed in his secure hold. *Try not to fight it.* They fell through the fresh scent of her blood. Mixed with the scents of pheromones that clung to them, the fresh erotic stew only added fuel to the pyromania gripping them. Rick knew what he'd do with a single thrust. The Drakken took control from him and lunged inside of her.

The Drakkens' voices blended in the night. The savage assault on both flesh and mind decimated any walls between them. Identities swirled in a maelstrom of emotions as the sentient beings finished what the humans started. There were no separate selves left. The parts fused into a whole.

The ground moved closer as they passed through curtains of vapor in the fall of a lifetime. Rick didn't know if he had time and distance to disengage before their bodies slammed into the ground. He dazedly regained power to open his wings. He kept Manny close and she allowed him to hold her.

The spikes retreated, but he maintained the sexual connection. He took them into a sweeping drive that slowed their momentum. He took his time with Manny, spotting a clearing between the trees where a brook added a ribbon of dancing condensation to the night. He put them down there, startling an early rising deer herd from their drink.

Rick eased her to the ground, pulled free of her arms and

reluctantly, her pussy. He looked at her, surprised when her bright eyes stared back at him. *I thought you'd passed out. You had me worried.*

Not at all, I was just lingering in the afterglow. She stretched on the ground, nearly taking the space from tree line to tree line. *I see the mental connection is stronger.*

How do you feel? Rick changed forms and went to his knees. He had no strength left. "Fuck, maybe we should have built up to marathon sex in the air." He checked his stomach. "You do realize you tried to gut me again."

Manny pulled her legs to her chest. The Drakken content to give control back to her. The shift made her gasp as pain rushed over every nerve system. Before she could scream it dissipated. She shook her head. "I think you're safe."

"I heard that gasp, are you okay?"

"Just a sharp pain, then it was gone when I shifted."

"How about other places?" He got to his feet and moved up to where she sat. The clearing seemed much bigger with them out of Drakken form. He thrust his hand down to her. "We need to get back to real light and check things out."

"I'm thirsty, but everything else seems okay." She took his hand and rose to her feet. They held each other in silence for a moment. "Thirsty." Manny pulled back as she reminded him.

"That's why I stopped here." He led her to the bank and they drank their fill. The false dawn passed into stygian black, the dark before the dawn fell around them. "We should get back."

"Go ahead." Manny waved him before her. "I'll follow you."

Rick studied her in the darkness. He saw her easily with the added senses of the Drakken. She wasn't the same woman who'd rushed off the edge of the cliff expecting the Drakken to follow orders. He nodded and released the human form. Heavy wing beats fluttered wind against the leaves as he took off.

Manny watched him. His superior attitude left no doubt. He knew he'd challenged her and beaten her. She bit her lips, denying the smile that wanted to bloom over her face. She could live with that. Rick circled the clearing again, clearly waiting on her. She took form and joined him. The smell of pine followed her where they'd disturbed the trees, needles fell in her wake. The cabin never looked so good as they winged their way toward it.

We didn't leave lights on. Rick's voice was hushed as it rode mental currents to her.

Only the fire.

Circle around west and meet me north. Rick tipped his wing and left her in steady flight.

CHAPTER 21

Manny followed his lead and rose higher. Her wings nearly silent, she watched the ground as she quartered her way to meet him. She didn't see anything and only then realized he'd sent her away from the road that led up to the cabin.

He was right to protect you.

He didn't give me a choice. Manny's emotions were so close to the surface anger shaded her words. Patience was gone.

When we are together it will be clear what mating, the claiming, means.

He'd better have a damn good excuse. Manny hadn't realized they'd automatically shut off the mental argument between them and Rick until he burst through the shield.

Are you okay?

The terse question both riled her anger and placated something inside her. *Of course*. She dropped toward him. He moved in a slow spiral.

I think it's Mitch. Something must be going on for them to get back up here.

Then let's go see what's blown up now. Manny turned directly for the cabin. Strong beats had her in the dooryard in moments. Not wanting to face whoever was at the cabin nude and human, she took the kin form and waited for Rick to come up beside her. Wrapped in his kin, he took the lead.

They went up the steps and pushed open the door. A quick search showed them a flash drive. *We have a couple problems*. Rick tossed her the drive. They shifted forms once more, grabbed clothes and retreated to the bathroom.

***

In the shower enclosure she received a spa treatment that curled her toes. Rick shampooed her hair and rinsed. He added conditioner and then piled the slippery mess on top of her head before he soaped her from head to foot.

"You are mine, I have mated you before all others. I live to care for you, I belong to you forever." He'd intoned the words softly. The rush of water covered every syllable of the promise.

Something inside her core tightened, and tears threatened when he went to his knees and pressed kisses against her belly. He'd just given her his vow, his marriage oath. His hands wrapped around the globes of her ass he held her to him. She found words from her Drakken to share with him. There had been no poetry in her soul until she'd accepted the wine colored beast that shared her body from blood to bone. Manny tugged him to his feet before going to her knees.

"You are mine. I claim you as mate and male until the seas dry to dust." Tears came then and she kissed his belly then cupped his cock and balls in her hands and left kisses over them.

"Fuck, yes." Rick's knees weakened and he caught her shoulders and helped her to her feet. He pushed her under the water to rinse and started soaping his body. He wanted her again. He needed a moment to seal the bond. He wanted to see her soul through her eyes and know she belonged to him, at long last.

Knowing there was trouble brewing around the mad scientist, Rick couldn't wait. They retreated out of the bathroom to the end bedroom. Mitch would have to cool his heels a little longer. He dried Manny slowly, looking every inch of flesh over for injuries. He pushed her to the mattress, parting her legs and searched the softest flesh for abuse. Her skin was perfect.

He left kisses and nips behind, smiling as chill bumps followed his shameless path.

By the time Rick got back to her mouth Manny's hands clenched tight the linens that covered the bed. He took her mouth and forced her jaws to part. She'd grind her teeth to enamel splinters if he didn't. He pulled away and watched her lick her lips. Whether she tasted him, licking him from her or searched for more of his taste he didn't know. Mesmerized by the pink tip of her tongue and how elegantly she'd played his dick made it kick between his thighs.

Rick fisted the length and let his gaze rove down her body. Her nipples peaked to hard points and he grasped one between his fingers. Lower, his gaze wandered to see the wet sheen that coated her swollen lips. Her pussy glistened with her want. His superior smile spread before he moved to get up close and personal with her clit and the sweetness that trickled from the portal below it. He dragged his tongue from bottom to top to collect her taste. He savored it a moment before taking her clit between his lips.

Manny arched at his contact. A long moan dragged from her throat, her hands fisted his hair, holding him closer she shivered, caught in her lust. She needed more from him. Pressure or a faster flick of his tongue on the center point of her pleasure. She'd take a bite from his sharp teeth if he'd just nudge her into the orgasm and let her come. "Please, Rick, now." Manny thrust her hips up but he pulled back.

"Oh, no. You scared me out there. I think you deserve a little punishment." He looked up the length of her undulating body to see the shock in her eyes. In less than a full breath anger lit the lovely colors, lighted the shades and elongated the pupil. There was the fire, yet he withheld the key to her orgasm.

Manny wasn't going to give in. She'd followed her Drakken's instructions to the letter. She trusted the creature to take care of her, always. The wild one knew the forces and worked with the Guardians of the Air. "I did nothing wrong."

"You and that great wine-colored beast scared years off my life." Rick whispered to her. Every syllable gusted against uber sensitive flesh, tantalizing the powerful orgasm that hovered out of reach.

Manny twitched and her next breath hitched in her chest. He scolded her, but his fingers worked inside her. Rick stretched two fingers deep inside and turned his wrist. The pads of his fingers stroked over her G-spot with purpose and the breath gusted from her.

Rick repeated the caress and watched her muscle strength desert her. A trembling mass on the covers, she squirmed with every move of his hand. He coaxed her to the edge, holding her there before stopping. Her skin dewed and her chest flushed up her throat to her cheeks. She broke her hold on the sheets, both hands moving to take control of her pleasure. He stopped that by clasping them in one of his. "Not so fast."

"Rick, please."

Her plaintive tone twinned with his female, his mate and Rick stopped the less than subtle torture. He moved up her body on his knees, parting her legs wider as he moved between them. Her hands he rested against the pillows, palms up. "Don't move a muscle." His demand echoed his Drakken and both females nodded, those wide radiant eyes a giveaway her Drakken hovered close.

He pulled his hand from her pussy and grabbed his dick. There was plenty of slick cream to coat his length. He gave a twirling pump to the rigid length. A drop of precum hovered on the tip and he mixed both on the next swipe from crown to balls. Releasing his dick, he pushed her knees wide then picked them up and pushed them to her hips. "You are so beautiful like this. Wide open and ready for me, you glow." He settled into the saddle of her body, one hand at her side, the other between them to stroke his cock from her ass to her clit. He swirled it around there, recoating her erect clit.

On the next pass he stopped and lodged the head in the portal he was about to claim. Her broken moan seized his attention and he locked her eyes with his. The full glow had returned. Her pupils were long and so very black they reflected his face. He held her hip and lunged. Seating his cock to the balls he stopped at the bottom.

Manny arched, her pussy stretched beyond pain. She bit her lip and tasted blood. The whip of sensation burned along her every nerve. She hungered, needed more of this. Her legs wrapped around his hips in response. "More." Her hands she kept extended above her head, but she watched his every move above her. The female inside her sought more of the pained pleasure, the purr loud in the room.

Rick pulled back, taking a deep breath as her pussy clutched around him. Every inch he withdrew lit fires along his veins, the pulses grasped him so tight. His balls tightened but he held onto the rush. He paused and held Manny down. "You're doing good with those hands." He nodded to her and then repeated the last movement. His hips jarred her body upward on the bed. Her breasts bounced from the force. The sound that left her throat this time was clear warning.

Manny curled under the lick of burn and stretched tissues. The ridge of his cock swept over the soft spot nestled behind her clit. Her gums ached and she clenched her jaw. “Kin.” Manny warned him as he pulled back, leaving her empty. She shifted into the larger form.

The flutter of magick over his skin forced him into changing. He seated his cock again. Grabbing her arms, he lifted her and set his ass on his heels. Manny took the last inches of his cock when her weight settled on his lap. She grunted and he kissed her.

Rick lifted her, reseated her, and waited until the waves of carnality eased. Her legs went around his waist. Her arms went around his neck and he cupped the cheeks of her ass to keep up the rhythm of thrust and withdraw. Manny’s body held him with furious convulsions, her clit continually stimulated by the hard ridge of his pubes.

The scent of her cream filled the air, a wreath around them of potent pheromones. The very essence of her clouded his thoughts and released the beast. The Drakken took over. His strength counterbalanced with his weight as he leaned back. The furious slap of bodies, the grunts, purrs, and growls of the wild ones filled the bedroom.

Rick held her, but his Drakken rode his mate. There was no room for humanity between the primeval creatures. Manny clawed his back and bit his shoulder in separate orgasms, or perhaps one long wave of pleasure took her mind. Rick grasped her hair and pulled her away from where she’d bitten his shoulder. He licked the blood from her lip and bowed her body over in a hard arc. The liquid pooled on his balls to run down his thighs to the bedding. He found a harsh, primal cadence that stimulated them both. *I won’t be long*.

Come. With. Me. Manny returned the thought.

Rick pulled her to him and struck her shoulder, sinking his teeth deep. The wash of pain shared through the mental connection destroyed his fragile hold. His cock swelled, the spikes emerged and he growled through the orgasm as it ripped through him. He seated deep within her and cupped her lower spine to keep her perfectly impaled.

CHAPTER 22

He let her blood coat his tongue as he exchanged fluids with her, his cock pumping as if it would never stop. Manny tightened in his arms, her pussy constricted around his cock. The very motions dug the savage spikes into her. He smelled her fresh sea musk and blood. Rick couldn't pull away, not until those damn spikes withdrew.

He lowered her to the bed. She hissed at the chill from the covers. A glance up showed sunrise. He eased his body over hers, supporting his weight on knees and elbows. "I love you." He kissed the shoulder he'd bitten, taking a few drops of her blood on his tongue. Her flesh already healed. He never appreciated the wonder of sex on their physical body.

"I believe you. I love you, Richard Carlisle."

"You keep saying my full name." He knew the instant the spikes slipped into his body. Manny transformed back to her human form. He was a second behind. He pulled free and staggered off the bed.

"I love all of you. Where are you going?" Manny went to her elbows to watch him, her gaze blurry. She'd never have made it to her feet after that round of orgasms.

"I know. That's why I went to get this." Rick smiled at her when he returned with a wash cloth and towel.

"You heard my thoughts?"

"The bond set between us as mates. Unless we wish not to hear, that connection is always open." Rick pushed one knee back to open her. He was gentle with the rough cotton. Her flesh radiated heat. Blood trickled from his favorite spot and her erect clit. He wiped the cotton along every inch to clean and soothe. He used the towel to dry and then tucked it between her legs.

He'd done a quick swipe of his dick and ball sac in the bathroom. He tossed the cloth through the door and got back in bed beside her. Manny rolled to face him and he took her in his arms, tucking her next to his body. She shivered as his body heat soaked into her. Due to the last shift, the only wounds on her skin were bruises, hickeys from his bite.

"I need to feed you," Rick told her while they drowsed.

"I am hungry," she muttered, half asleep.

"Then get dressed. I'll meet you in the kitchen."

***

Dressed and seated at the table, they pushed empty plates away. Manny clutched her coffee cup, he gaze directed down as she thought over what Mitch's brief covered. "We'd been so close."

"Not what scares me. The sick bastard bred children from his toxic soup." Rick kicked back from the table as he stood. "He needs to be wiped off the face of the earth." He took her plate with his to the sink and lowered them with a clatter.

"What do we do with more children?" She looked up at him as he turned to face her. His features hard and emotionless. She could have guessed the words before he spoke them.

"We'll make sure they follow their creator straight to hell."

***

Laurel kicked the trashcan and cursed. He'd figured Mitch would find him, although he'd hoped for more time. Oh, well. The test subjects were still in his possession and the lab Mitch and his misfits discovered hadn't told them much.

"You're sure they didn't find anything of interest." He turned to the twins.

"There was nothing here when I left last night, Doctor." Senoia assured him.

"We sanitized every particle we left behind for them to find. There is no way they could piece together our location." Spencer shook his head. "We shut down the bounce trail before ending transmission. We cleared out everything by flash drive and then cannibalized the hard drives, crippled the motherboards." Spencer crossed his arms over his chest, proud he'd taken care of all of that for the doctor. "They know nothing."

Dr. Emerson Laurel wanted to smile at the youth's boast, except Laurel had tangled with Mitch and his special force before. They were smarter than this wet-behind-the-ears youngster. Spencer certainly had the skills, Laurel had to admit. He bit his lips to keep the admiration in. "We have things to do today. Senoia, is the lab set up as you need?"

"Yes, doctor. Everything is perfect. As soon as we're through here, I'll be heading over to get to work. I want to recheck that anomaly you found."

"Good girl, see that you do. Spencer, I want to speak with you. Please join me for breakfast."

Spencer and Senoia glanced at each other. He'd been a wonderful boss, and what he'd taught them they'd spend years otherwise acquiring the knowledge. "Of course, Dr. Laurel."

"Excellent. Off you go, Senoia. Make sure the hired help is taking diligent care of our charges."

Senoia left without an answer. Her employer didn't expect one. He'd already turned that great mind of his in another direction. That was fine with her. She'd gotten his text this morning after a sleepless night. She'd gotten lost in the side streets of Atlanta and met a gorgeous if dangerous man to ask directions.

She'd wondered on her way home if he had a gentle brother, maybe one that didn't look to shoot a stranger in the street. He'd stirred her libido. That much raw power, the otherworldly spell he cast upon her lingered through a shower and glass of wine. He'd entertained her thoughts until her current job took over.

They were keeping two orphans. They didn't have birth certificates. She knew Laurel hadn't registered them. They were invisible. She understood some of it, but they'd have to have public identities sooner or later. She hopped onto her scooter. She didn't need a car to park. It was difficult getting through constant construction and blocked streets as it was. Parking was a total nightmare on its own.

She zipped past traffic and around the back of the new building. It wasn't that far from her apartment or the old lab. She walked the scooter to the back door and punched in the combination. Opening it, she pushed the bright red ride inside. The door closed behind her, so well maintained only the whisper of sound as it met the concrete reached her ears. Senoia dug her backpack from the seat compartment. Tossing it over her shoulder, she moved through the garage space and into the lab proper. She heard raised voices coming down the hallway and hurried down to see what was happening.

"We have two infants who need identification." The midwife stood bent over, hands on her hips as she made her statement through clenched teeth. Her head and neck stretched out, a flush on her face, this was far from the start of the argument.

"They belong to Laurel. His to do with. We have nothing to say in this matter."

"You have lost your friggin' mind. There are laws and regulations." Exasperation filled her tone, delivered with frustration.

"Ladies." Senoia halted the confrontation. "How are the boys today?" They'd had to order extra furniture. One of the infants set the bedding on fire after the nurse ignored him for too long. They'd let him cry, of course. It had been a scientific hunch the doctor played.

The other clearly loved the water, so much so that bath time was a challenge for anyone involved. The creatures could transform at will. The water Drakken changed into an adorable lizard. Cue the splashing and water play.

"Both are doing well." The nurse reported after she sent a disdainful glare at the midwife. "Their appetites are growing. They've not lost a pound. They're alert and content."

"Good to hear." Senoia glanced at the midwife. "You have an issue with how the doctor is handling his charges?"

The woman paled and shook her head. "Not at all, Doctor Knyght. Everything is fine." She shook her head. "I believe I'm developing a migraine. If you are here perhaps I could have the rest of the day off?"

"You may." Senoia loved hearing the word doctor from the midwife's lips. She'd worked hard in her field and deserved the honor. Besides, with the midwife gone they could take the samples and set up the studies Laurel wanted today.

She didn't wait until the woman cleared the door. Reaching into her bag, Senoia slipped out a sheet of paper and handed it to the nurse. "I want to start with the water one." Senoia turned on her heel, knowing the nurse would obey. She walked into the lab, taking a deep breath. *Yes, this* is *what I love to do*.

She donned a lab coat and readied the instruments.

CHAPTER 23

What do you think happened?

I don't know. The fight ended.

I'm Kelby, first born son of water. He'd only caught glimpses of his fellow Drakken.

I'm Haydn, son of fire.

Their connection strengthened as they used it. BJ helped them with speech and he'd taught them how to hide all thoughts from the adult caregivers. They sensed one other and wondered when they would meet. The link between Kelby and Haydn snapped apart when Kelby sensed someone close by. Both infants dropped strong instinctive shields to hide their abilities.

***

Rick cruised from the mountains to the tiny town the team called home. The day was partly cloudy and the wind sweet. Spring arrived with a soft hello. It made the trip on the cycle easy to enjoy.

Instead of turning off toward his house he bypassed the road and continued. He passed Manny's little cottage. Their destination was Mitch's fortress in the field. He roared up the drive and parked. When Manny eased her arms from around his chest he missed the warmth of contact. The door opened and Regina waved them into the house.

Manny took of the helmet. "Guess the cookout has started."

Rick followed her example. He put it down on the seat. "Sounds like it from what I can hear." Distant music filled the air in counterpoint with laughter. A tension he hadn't noticed eased. His Drakken relaxed along with him. He held out his hand, aware that Regina watched them from the door. "Let's go get this over with."

He smiled at her, his eyes flashing the long pupil.

Manny's lips twisted, she couldn't smile yet. She satisfied herself it was a start. She slipped her hand into his and walked with him up to the house. "Hi, Regina."

"Hello, Manny. Looks like the cabin was a good place to stop. Or start."

"Yes, ma'am, it was." Rick grinned, his accent coming out in every word.

They thought he'd tuck Manny under his arm, against his side, a sure sign of their mated status. Rick waved Manny before him, released her hand, and then simply followed Regina into the house. She closed and locked the door. Habit by now. "Everyone's in the back yard, I'm sure you heard them. Manny could you help me with something in the kitchen?"

Rick felt her tense. He paused in his trek and looked back at her.

Manny shook her head once, her hands locked together in front of her. "Won't be a minute."

"I'll be waiting." A dominant thread filled his voice. The answer became an order she dare not ignore. She did smile this time and pushed him toward the back of the house.

"Go on, I'll see you in a sec." Rick left her. She watched his broad shoulders block out the light from the back door. Before he exited she turned on her heel and joined Regina in the kitchen.

"You don't seem to be the worse for wear. Either of you." Regina piled buns, a stack of cheese and condiments on a tray.

"It was close. I nearly gutted him. Then the Drakken took her turn." Manny shrugged. "We got through the worst of it. Then went back again."

"Both of you are okay?" Regina paused and looked hard at the operative.

Manny wanted to squirm under her steady regard. Regina knew what they'd done. She'd participated in the dive herself. Still, it wasn't a subject Manny wanted to discuss now, maybe not ever. "How about you grab that bottle of red wine and after that maybe we can talk about it."

Regina glanced over her shoulder, grabbed the bottle in question and added it to the tray. They picked up everything and headed toward the noise and food.

***

Haydn, do you know the other two? Kelby had kept his silence for a long time. Their existence had changed since they'd entered this world of noise and light.

No. I do know one is like us. His name is BJ.

The other one, you sense him close, too? He'd been trying to figure out who the shadow was. The telepathic touch had given away almost nothing. His mental sign was older than the infants. It frustrated Kelby.

He isn't close like the caregivers. He's away, but he's watching. Haydn's voice was strong.

Kelby didn't know how. He was exhausted. That was how he felt the outsider's mental touch. He'd been handled until his skin throbbed, a sensitive feeling that made his belly ache.

Good thing we're together. Kelby told Haydn before he fell into sleep.

***

"I don't see any lasting injuries." Mitch made the soft comment as Rick strolled past him to get a beer from the cooler.

"All is well, Commander." Rick didn't slow his steps. He had a feeling he might need a couple of those icy beers before the night was over. He'd glanced around the patio before stepping out. Everyone was there. James carried an alert BJ around in a sling. Tracy was under the umbrella at the table, scrolling through her phone.

Gareth and Mike were tossing a plastic disk in the yard. Rick paused a moment to watch. He hadn't done that since they'd used them in BUD/S training. Watching them race and leap to catch it brought back memories. Some of them not so nice. He popped the top of the beer and swallowed half without tasting the cold brew.

"You guys make it out okay?" James distracted him, and Rick left them to their play.

"Sure. A little scratch here and there, but we're good," Rick assured him. "BJ's growing like a weed."

"Doc said he's put on the pounds that Tracy's losing."

"Good for her." Rick nodded to Tracy. "She looks really good, James."

"Hey, Rick. Seems like I never see you anymore," Max Williams interrupted. He'd been studying burgers on the grill when Rick walked out. The men clasped hands.

"'Cause you collect airplanes like I buy bikes." They chuckled. Max was the only flyboy on the team. There hadn't been many Air Force *Below*.

"I do. Have the sweetest retro Cherokee."

Rick held up his hand. "Let me stop you there, my brother."

Max shook his head but pulled out his phone to show off a few pictures. "It needs a little work."

Rick shook his head as he looked at the derelict plane. "That needs to be retired. You and a team of mechanics and body work pros couldn't put that humpty POS back together."

"What piece of shit are you talking about?" Derryck leaned in between them. He glanced at the phone and whistled low. "I get it."

"Good to see you, man." Rick bumped fists with his friend.

"Happy to be here." Derryck drifted away as quickly as he'd appeared.

Rick crushed the empty in his fist and went to get another beer. Max returned to the grill. At another table Ben and Trevor conversed, heads close, voices too soft to hear. He saw Manny and Regina come from the house and moved to take the tray from Manny.

"Time to eat." Regina called to the pair on the lawn. Max walked over with a platter of meats. The time for talk and visiting were over for now.

***

"I know you want to get to business. I'll leave you to it." Regina stood with her glass in hand.

"Wait for me." Tracy plucked BJ out of his father's arms and dropped a quick kiss on James's lips. "See you in a few."

"You bet," James whispered back.

Mike followed the women. As a research tech, he didn't have much to add to the coming meeting. Gareth grabbed his hand and put a kiss in the palm. Mike smiled and closed his hand.

"Okay, folks. Here's what we've found." Mitch slid several folders onto the table. Several hands reached for them, opened the files, and started scanning.

Rick tapped a photo in his file. "I just saw this girl." Mutters ceased and all eyes turned to him. Rick flipped the photo around.

"She'd gotten lost in Atlanta, by that famous hotdog stand, you know the one I mean?" Several men nodded. "She asked directions, but it seemed to me she came out of nowhere. I was leaving the bar and didn't see a soul." Rick started the picture around the table. No one else recognized her.

"You think maybe she was leaving the lab?" Mitch leaned forward, elbows on the table.

"I don't know. Maybe. She had on a jacket, I think. Had a messenger bag strapped across her chest." Rick shook his head. He'd had too much to drink that night, so the edge of his memory blurred.

"I think maybe we need to check out that side street," Mitch told them. "I'll get Jake on it. He can search the blocks around the area to see if our mad scientist left a blank spot." He stood and left them with the other files.

There wasn't much else to add. Emerson Laurel had escaped both the fed and local agencies and the Brotherhood. What the authorities didn't know was that he'd taken two very pregnant women with him on the run.

"Think he has babies?" Trevor brought to light what everyone was thinking.

"Probably." Max was glum. "Those two innocents in that monster's hands makes me wanna puke."

"You're not the only one, Max." Ben put his hand on Max's arm. "The guardians are working with them. One is fire and one water, both are males." He glanced at the back door, where a protective Tracy just took her son. "I don't doubt BJ has spoken with them and they to him."

"They can do that?" Trevor spoke again.

"BJ showed me pictures only a day after his birth of what happened in the house that day." James shrugged. He hadn't had time to come to terms with nearly losing the love of his life. "He helped us find her."

"But ain't that like a mother and child thing?" Trevor looked around the assembly. "That's all researched and proven, right?"

"Yes, Trevor. But here we're dealing with something outside the realm of most natural science studies." Ben chuckled at Trevor's lost look. "Here be Drakkens and magick and guardians of the elements who combine into an extreme team."

"I'm not ready to face all that." Trevor crossed his arms over his chest and shook his head. He stared hard at Manny. "You were all like that, as I remember." It came out accusatory. He'd believed every word she'd used to lie to the team. He wasn't ready to forgive her.

Last week he couldn't wait to shift forms and train. This week he had a hard-on against the turn her life had taken. Manny shook her head. He was always blowing hot and cold. How she put up with him she didn't know. It just seemed somehow they clicked and it worked. Rick took her hand under the table.

CHAPTER 24

Manny's gaze turned to Derryck. He'd been the most damaged when rescued from *Below*. He was better now with the Regina working with him. The marine was normally closed mouth, the epitome of tall, dark, handsome with the added silent type. She watched him with the 8x10 glossy. She'd memorized the girl's features, but not like Derryck seemed to be doing.

"You think they're trying to communicate?" Derryck asked, he held the photo of the girl in his hand. One fingertip stroked the long black run of her hair. Her eyes tipped up at the outside. It gave a feline cast to her features. She had beautiful tanned skin and rosy cheeks. The slight smile exposed white even teeth. Those lips beckoned his touch, fed his need to kiss. He raked his lower lip against his teeth. He'd missed the conversation and forced himself to tune in.

"I believe we'll be able to use them to pin-point the location better than Jake did," Ben finished as Mitch came from the house with a tablet in his hand.

"What are they cussing me for now?" Jake's plaintive voice came from the speaker. The entire assembly laughed. "Better how?" He waited while the guys wound down.

"I was just telling them if BJ is telepathic and able to shift, he may be the one to find the others better than you'll be able to." Ben explained.

"Not so, Mr. Magick. I happen to have the address of the current digs of that crazy bastard." That got everyone's attention. They leaned forward, eager for Jake's input.

"Go ahead," Mitch told Jake.

"Rick was right. She has a place around the corner. She was on foot but could use transportation. Figuring she was lost in thought and missed a connecting road to her home, I found three 'dead spaces'."

"What's a dead space?" Leave it to Trevor.

"It's where an address exists, with tax information and a sale or lease stamp in the local realtor listing. The property says it's unoccupied currently but up for viewing. Cross check that with the postal service and other delivery services. There are deliveries that can be traced back to the address in question over the last few weeks." There were keystrokes over the tablet then Jake came back. "Just like that one. Someone signed electronically for a delivery of five cases of diapers, six cases of formula and a gross of baby wipes, Boss," He stopped. "less than thirty minutes ago."

"I need that address." Mitch looked around the table. "We're on the road. I want two three-man teams. James, you're with Max and Trevor."

James nodded and got to his feet. He'd go in to tell Tracy.

"Manny, you take Rick and Gareth." Mitch stared at her long enough she fidgeted.

"Yes, Boss."

"If anything comes up—" He shifted his glance to encompass the others. Rick nodded and Gareth smiled.

"What could possibly happen? She likes things that go boom and now she's full Drakken." Gareth looked at her and winked.

Manny managed a deeper breath and a tip of her head. She wasn't ready for smiles and congratulations. The team seemed to sense that and they respected it. They respected her. It was another unusual warm fuzzy feeling.

They all got to their feet. "Derryck and John, I want your eyes on the civilians."

"Don't let Reggie hear that." John Moody seemed to be settling down.

"Don't tell her I said that. We'll explore the other places first. The apartments on the two new techs. Look for more information on the nurse and the other woman taking shifts with the infants."

Most of the team headed inside, and Jake signed off the computer to gather what extras he could for them. "Hey, Mitch." The call stopped him mid-stride. He turned to face Max.

"What is it?"

"The infants?"

"We'll try to take them alive. Regina has some experience with BJ. I doubt the mad scientist wants to dissect them. If he bred Drakken children, then we need to keep this to ourselves. He won't get the chance to enslave them or sell them to interested bidders."

"Good to know." He nodded, but something more bothered him. Mitch hadn't said they were out of danger.

"If it comes to a bad end, we'll take care of them." Mitch's voice dropped and chilled. The team that hadn't been *Below* called this particular tone the chill of death. Manny and Rick exchanged a look.

Max released the tension he'd been holding, his shoulders dropped and he exhaled a deep breath. "Good to know."

Mitch clapped him on the back.

***

Nightfall in Atlanta was never dark. There were shadows around of course. The constant bustle of traffic, occasional horns, the laughter of afterhours clubs loading and unloading customers kept the sidewalks and streets busy. The teams deployed with final instructions. Mitch kept contact from a distance. The teams wore small cameras at their shoulders, thanks to Jake.

Manny glanced at Rick. Shades blending into the night, they were going after the personnel. James's team was on the infants. She nodded. Gareth stepped up and rapped smartly on the door. They waited, tense. Manny had unscrewed the bulbs in the hallway earlier. They'd found no independent cameras. This would be a grab and go. They had questions and this suspect had answers. The door opened.

"Yes?"

"Hello, I need you to come with me." Gareth looked over her head to see if anyone else was home.

"Is there something wrong?" She quickly grabbed a purse from the side table and a set of keys. She hooked a sweater in her hand and stepped out. The door locked automatically behind her.

Manny rolled her eyes. Laurel wasn't very careful with the new hired hands. Guess he figured they were safer buried in the big city.

"I need to you come along." Gareth intimidated her and she

clearly gave into his authority. She asked no other question, even when she detected two dark silhouettes at the head of the stairs. Rick kept deep into the shadows so she wouldn't recognize him. The black cap on his head helped. They escorted her out of the building and into Mitch's SUV.

Manny shut the door and jogged up the street. They'd found out the two techs were twins, last name Knyght. Her brother was easy to find after that bit of information. He was just as trusting as his sibling. They slid together in the back seat. The doors were childproofed. If they'd tried to get out the doors wouldn't open.

"I want you to get this straight between you." Mitch told her in his rough voice.

"We're good." Manny's voice faded as Mitch shook his head in negative.

"The bond isn't set. Your Drakken are together but not complete. You're still at loose ends about some things. I can sense it, so can the others." She glanced across the seat where Gareth stared out the windshield. If he'd heard any of the conversation he wasn't giving anything away.

"Sir." Manny's stomach tightened. Had they let the team down some way? Were they not as effective as team members should be? The uncertainties multiplied and she dropped her eyes to hide the guilt and shame growing at the rush of thought.

"Fix it. Then come back to us." Manny watched Mitch drive away. Rick stood at her back.

"What now?" she asked Rick. They'd stashed their bikes in a more public part of town just a short walk away. She pulled off her cap and stuffed it into the cargo pocket of her BDUs. Unbuttoning the jacket, she tightened the ties and left it to hang open, exposing the neon pink shirt under it. Nothing she could do to disguise the bottom of her BDUs or her boots. Her mind swirled, she'd have to tell Rick.

"I want to head back out to the cabin." He grabbed her and tugged her closer to his side. "You know, where you can make all the noise you want when we get together?"

"I know." Manny sighed and brushed her hand through the loose strands of her hair. No matter how tightly she braided it there were always escapees. "Mitch said we weren't done as Drakken. The others know we're not done."

"How the hells would they know?" Rick glanced after the SUV, long gone now.

Manny shrugged. "Mitch wouldn't lie to us. We're not finished in a way the others know."

Rick's heart tightened, threatened to stop altogether at her defeated expression. Her features looked drawn with guilt. "Look. I know a place. It's close and there are no neighbors."

Manny looked at him. "Where is this mythical place in the heart of Atlanta?"

"See, it's not here. Just a few minutes outside the city. Half an hour tops. With Mitch telling us we're off duty he won't need us until he calls us in. The other team is ready to go." He held his breath, waited for her commitment to them, to the finish. She made him wait.

"Okay. I'll follow you."

CHAPTER 25

"Where are the children?" Mitch backed into an alley, shifted into park and leaned his arm over the back of the seat. He had the other team ready for retrieval. They needed to know where.

The twins looked at each other, eyes wide in the darkness, The whites reflected the glow of neon that lit the city. "We aren't to tell."

"Let me explain something." Mitch took a breath. He knew the intimidation factor of his ruined voice. He wasn't above using it as a weapon. The fire dragon took care of his vocal cords long ago. "I want those assets in my custody. They will not be auctioned off to the highest bidder. They will not be used in the advancement of Laurel's super soldier experimentation. They will not be kept as lab rats for further examination. You will not torture them, sequester them, or sell them." Mitch watched the girl shiver, her gaze glued to her hands twisting in her lap.

"Doctor Laurel is a great scientist." Spencer had to clear his throat before words formed. His tone wasn't as strong as he'd thought it should be. Still, he felt he had to defend the scientist.

"Where are the assets?" Mitch ground out between his teeth. His eyes shifted to his Drakken red, pupils elongated. The latent glow lit their faces. Senoia gasped and Spencer took her hand. He gave the address of the nursery without hesitation.

"Team Two, have the mailbox of the assets." Gareth called the other team waiting for this information.

"Team One, go," Max answered the call, then looked at James behind the wheel. He jotted down the address and signed off. "We're off." James started the engine, Max put in the address.

Trevor kept his silence as James put the SUV in motion, his eyes on traffic as they pulled away from the last triangulation where Jake suggested them take.

"They'll be fine in the seats?" Max didn't fidget but his voice held the uncertainty.

"Safe as a bug – dot dot dot. You know how that goes?" James told him turning into the parking lot of a deserted manufacturing structure.

"Damn, you don't think they're safe here do you?" Max stared into the shadows. James had already turned off the lights, sneaking in dark and as slowly as possible to be silent. They stopped the roll forward but James didn't shift into park. They'd have no time to change direction with babes in their arms. He reversed the SUV then shifted and turned the key. Silence, at least the silence of a bustling city engulfed them.

"We're go." Max muttered into the mic. They got out of the dark vehicle and made their way into the compound. Trevor led, smaller and less encumbered by weapons. Inside the building, finding no alarm system, they blinked against the lights. A voice claimed their attention, James nodded Trevor forward.

Trevor took a dart from his pocket, inserted it into a small blowgun. His new baby delighted him and he'd been practicing for weeks. He didn't hesitate to give the single puff, landing the small dart full of anesthetic exactly where he wanted. The woman's knees buckled and he rushed forward to catch her.

"Wha—" the woman's eyes rolled up and she sagged in his hold. He put her on the floor, a quick nod to his team.

"I'll get on the info dump. You guys find the kids." He took his dart from her neck and put it away in his bag. "She'll be out for another hour at least." They nodded and moved past the doorway. Trevor rose to his feet and walked out of the room, the cup of coffee she'd been waiting for in her hand.

You're going to be taken, by my father. Keep quiet and all will be well. BJ told the boys. He'd listened to his mother and the doctor here speak of the mission. *Soon we'll be able to meet.* There was some excitement in his tone and the other boys thrilled at his words.

Steps sounded in the hallway and the boys kept still.

"At least they housed them together." Max told James. They

paused at the window to look into the next room on the silent tour. Luckily it was the nursery. Or a room set up as one. Boxes of diapers and formula were stacked on one wall. The opposite held a sink, one better fit to a restaurant than a nursery. Changing tables bumped against the deep steel wall.

"This one is Baby Boy 1." Max's voice held contempt. "He didn't even give them names." He gathered the little body and picked him up. He paused and picked up the clipboard at the foot of the bassinet. A glance at the info and he tucked it into the pouch on his pants.

"BJ will let us know. Make sure you have him wrapped securely." James/ gaze crawled over the walls and ceiling, looking for any sign of a camera. Strange the mad scientist hadn't kept a remote eye on his next experiment. He wrapped the baby in the blanket and lifted his little body to nestle against his chest. "Hang in there."

The nurse is around. One of the boys spoke to James, mind to mind. *She doesn't leave us for long.*

She's taking a little nap. You need not worry.

You are BJ's father.

Yes and we're here to take you home.

The little one said nothing more that James heard.

Max followed James from the room, keeping an eye out for any rear ambush. The baby fit against him, the tiny body cradled along his forearm. They collected Trevor, hands full of drives and a couple tablets. He stored them in hidden pockets around the belt he wore with his BDUs.

They slipped out the way they'd come in.

The SUV James drove had two infant seats in the back. Trevor moved between them as Max and James buckled the babies in. They got into the front and James turned over the powerful engine.

"Was that too easy?" Trevor asked, glancing between the babies. Both faced him in the rear facing car seats. Their eyes reflected their disquiet, long pupils obvious. "It's okay boys, we're the good guys. You don't know it yet, but you'll catch on quick."

"No. It's never too easy," Max grumbled from the front seat.

"Tracy and Regina are ready for these little guys. We're about four hours from home. I hope they don't get hungry." James navigated the city streets easily and slipped into highway traffic quickly.

"It's the middle of the night." Trevor stated. "They should go to sleep, right?"

"From what this says in the last entry, both had bottles less than an hour ago." Max studied the notes on the clipboard then looked at James. "Think we're going to need formula and bottles?" They'd taken a couple boxes of diapers and several stacks of wipes, everything Trevor could carry.

Trevor, used everyone overlooking him, listened from the back. He kept busy making faces at the infants. There were toys with bells and feathers hanging from the handles of the seats. He flicked them to make them swing. The boys didn't focus on them, but it was something to distract them while the SUV melted into the ribbons of late night commuters.

"Where are you, Commander?" James's slip betrayed his nerves.

"Marker two-sixty." Mitch answered over the radio. "Everything okay with you?"

"Smooth in and out." He glanced at Max and cleared his throat. "We may need to make a little shopping run."

Dead silence hovered over the radio. Then Mitch rejoined them. "I take it there were no baby go-bags in sight."

"Right." James heard the laughter in Mitch's voice. He couldn't wait until the commander and his mate discovered they were having a child. James would bet the superior tone would change then.

"Noted."

James hoped the babies would go three to four hours without another feeding. If Trevor guessed right they might even sleep a few hours. He set the cruise control and headed north. They'd be home in four hours. If the kids could hang on that long everything was just minutes away. Including diaper changes and their next warm meal.

***

Rick led Manny down a dirt road. The bushes alongside overgrew the bare ruts and she ducked to miss a few of the larger ones. The last thing she wanted was to be swept off her bike. The ruts rambled over a mile and then made a sharp left turn up a slight rise. Higher they drove until the headlights revealed a yard that needed mowing and a house born in the nineteenth century.

Manny shut off her bike and stared at the two-story manor. More rustic than Mitch's cabin, from the outside it looked like it had seen a century of better days. She hoped the inside was more modern than the façade.

"I know it looks a little run down." Rick walked up beside her. She hadn't gotten off her bike. "Inside I've had it completely renovated. I don't have the contacts Mitch has, but there are a few surprises." He looked at the façade. "My great grandfather built this for the love of his life. Two generations of my family were raised here." He turned to her and took her hand to help her off the bike. He was a bit surprised she took the offer and swung her leg over the seat.

"It isn't much to look at." Rick glanced around the cleared but overgrown property. "Its closest neighbor is over a mile away as the crow flies." He led the way to the porch and slid aside a panel that looked to her like another weird tacked-on piece of siding. Under the board was a state of the art keypad. He had to allow print recognition then punch in the correct code. The door clicked. Manny thought it sounded metal. She touched it as it swung closed behind her. No squeaky hinges here. It was heavy duty.

The lights came on as Rick moved to his right. A dining table shared the room with a wood burning stove. Across the room was the kitchen, a long galley set up. Shelves lined one side and the sink, fridge, and stove stood on the other. Behind the wood stove was another room. Through the door she glimpsed a desk and chair.

The door opened in a small foyer. Stairs loomed straight ahead. The dining room sat on the right, and to the left was a sitting room. She put her helmet on the stair tread and her bag beside it. The lighting was lower here, but the comfort beckoned her like a loved one. She didn't resist. Claiming the most comfortable looking of the several chairs scattered around, she stared at the wall opposite as Rick exposed another electronic pad.

A flat screen dropped from the ceiling. "The satellite has over two hundred channels." He walked over to her and took the chair next to her. "We can veg for a while. I'll cook dinner and then see what happens." He kissed her knuckles. When she shivered and her gaze locked on him, he thrust his tongue between her fingers. Her pupils widened and her breath quickened. Satisfied, he released her.

Manny wanted more, so she took it. She darted to her feet and grabbed the back of his shirt. Hauling him backwards, she used the slight advantage and forced him to his knees, exactly where she wanted him. He'd called the tune ever since mating. She wanted to lead a dance now and again.

She stepped across his lower legs, her hand moving to fist in his hair. A tug pulled his head back. She studied him for a long time, seeing his features and adjusting to the changing insights she gleaned from them. She noticed his breathing quickened at first, but now settled down to strong regular sighs.

His features flushed as she watched. He licked his lips and she leaned down to take them. She took his upper lip between hers. His taste bloomed on her tongue as she swiped from side to side. She nipped the flesh and moved immediately to his bottom lip. That one she nibbled the length before a swipe of her tongue caressed him. She kissed him full on, invading his mouth and taking control. She shared the pain as she pressed their lips against his teeth. His jaw flexed and she moved inside. No surface was safe from her exploration.

Fisting his hair, she didn't let him drive into her kiss. She pressed his lips open and assaulted every surface. She curled her tongue around his, sucking it into her mouth before biting it to hold him there. She suckled the organ and relished his moan. His arms wrapped around her thighs, holding her close.

She lifted one leg to break his hold and curled the same leg around his side. She placed her foot down on his calf, allowed a bit of her weight to hold there. He grunted and she bit his tongue. Not hard enough to bring blood but to remind him she wanted control. His other arm dropped and he nodded.

She left his mouth so her lips could tour his cheek to his ear. She bit the lobe and then suckled the flesh. His shiver pleased both females. Without releasing his head, she moved it forward and bit the back of his neck, over the top of his spine. He shuddered under her sensual assault and a smile came naturally to her face. Sucking the tight flesh, she made sure there would be a reminder of her claim on him. The raspberry spot on the back of his neck made the Drakken within surface.

Manny stepped around him to pull his shirt up. She fought the material tightly tucked into his pants before it released and bunched in her fists. She pulled it over his head, dragging his arms straight up to help.

"Hold them there." Manny moved before him with the order. She went to her knees and pulled the web belt free with a clatter. The ends dropped and her hands went to the button fly. In no time she'd gotten his pants unfastened and pushed down his hips. His cock sprang free and a frisson of excitement lit her nerves.

She loved the length of him. The width of his cock spoke of the power and strength in the long shaft. She cupped him in her palm, closing her fingers around the circumference. Just the touch of him made her pussy slick while her inner muscles grasped at nothing. She'd change that in a few minutes. Manny wasn't through with him, not by a long shot. "Stand up, take off your boots and remove your pants." Crossing her arms, she moved away from him, eyes never leaving him.

CHAPTER 26

Rick was in his own personal hell. He followed her directions to the letter. Inside his head, his skin, the Drakken alternately laughed at the predicament and then purred with delight. Rick moved to his feet and felt a little uncomfortable untying his boots. Bare ass in the air, nearly upside down, he felt the blood rush to his face. He got the laces loose, kicked out of the boots and pushed the pants back down and off his feet.

He straightened. His dick wept and the head flared. He waited on her next directive. Damn if this wasn't the sexiest seduction he'd ever been involved in. He reached to grasp his dick, but her hand slapped his back to his side. His sassy mate wanted him at her mercy.

"I say when you touch your cock." She walked around him, her hand out and in contact with his waist. The bulge of muscle there invited her caress. Behind him, she let her fingers drift over the slope of his ass cheeks. She watched chill bumps cover the bare flesh. It wasn't cold in the room. She kept the satisfaction from showing on her face. She completed her tour of him. She liked seeing him on the floor in front of her. Her Drakken seemed less than thrilled, but she was warming up to the very thought of the male in such a submissive pose and mind set.

He's curbed his strength for you.

He will bow to my will whenever it's needed. Manny responded.

You needed to know that? The Drakken didn't sound sure of the statement.

Manny ran her fingers through his already mussed hair. Her

fingertips skimmed his eyebrows, followed the bony orbit around his eye. He watched her. Those unblinking hazel eyes missed nothing. *I did need to know that.* Manny took a breath. Rick allowed her to be anything she wanted to be. He gave her the room to explore everything she hadn't known about herself.

"On your back on the bed." She barked the command. Gratification filled her when there was no hesitation. She'd guessed right. Rick would stand beside her as mate. He'd support her from behind when there was need yet remain at her side as an equal. Things inside of her shifted. Some lived deep within her brain, some existed in the physical realm. She stilled to allow the new template time to settle over her. Pain, an animal shadow that existed soul deep, eased. The relief as painful as the possession flooded her system and Manny gasped. Tears filled her eyes. This time there was no guilt, no pain, no attempt to block the flow.

"Manny?" Propped on his elbows, Rick watched her. She glanced at him, his concern like warm gravy over the perfect buttered biscuit.

"I didn't say anything about speaking." Manny kept her voice a quick lash. Laughter, pure delight filled her and she tipped her head back and released it. Tears made tracks over her cheeks and Rick likely thought she was mad. "I'm fine."

She got busy with her clothes. Her body craved his in a way that transcended a simple sexual encounter. She was new, inside if not outside. There was anguish. The echo resounded within her, but it no longer caused her any pain. She was free and there were no words to describe the newness of being reborn into something so new.

She moved between his legs and posed on her knees. Her ass rested on her heels. She was bare before him as she'd never been. Well, there had been once, long ago. She shook her head. All reminders of her father tumbled from her brain, from her life. Her future lay before her. Long hard legs, knobby knees, up-thrust cock waited for her touch, her taste. Manny dove in. He'd gotten his look at her body.

Biting his left leg in short intervals, she moved up to his thigh. The muscle twitched but he didn't move otherwise. She turned to the right, started higher up. She licked the scar across the top. The edges were rough. She glanced up his body to meet his stare. There was no color left. Black encompassed the orb with the edges barely painted with green. The color there glowed, an emerald corona split with obsidian.

She moved up his body, stalking movements, a cat prowling the vast real estate of her bonded Drakken mate, her dragon lover. Manny inhaled the core of him. The scent drenched her senses with essential Rick. She lapped the newest pearl from the slit of his cock. One musky drop clung to the edge of the crown. Others already rolled down the shaft, leaving trails of opalescent glimmers down the slightly curved length.

Manny wrapped her hand around him. Using a twist, she worked his shaft until his hips lifted from the bed. Smiling, something she seemed to be doing a lot, she stuck out her tongue and released him. Starting at the base, she moved upwards, using her tongue to touch every surface. His flavor exploded on the sensory organ and she closed her eyes as bliss filled her. This, for her, all was right in her world.

"Pixie, um, if you keep—ouch, motherfucker!"

Manny bit him. Then she sucked him deep inside the warmth of her mouth, using her tongue to soothe the bite. He shuddered at the unexpected attack and she relished the power, the absolute control over him. In return, she received freedom she'd never experienced. She moved higher on his body, lining her hips with his. She grasped the heat and power of his cock. Her hand grasped him at the base. Cream collected from him coated the wide head as she guided him to the core of her body. With a sigh, her weight bore her down, impaling her on the shaft that stretched the tight channel. She stopped at the stretch, the lick of pain she was starting to enjoy.

"Rick, put your hands on my waist." Manny made small undulations with her hips without pulling away.

He couldn't stop the hiss of lust as every nerve came online. Rick followed her order, wrapping his hands around her waist. He'd thought nothing would be greater than the feel of her mouth taking him deep. He was wrong. She'd taken every inch of him into a full sensory surround. The head of his dick pressed against her cervix and every millimeter of her pussy massaged him from balls to tip.

Her hip movements tightened her pussy around him. He

wasn't going to last long. He tried to think of distractions. Coffee, mowing the grass, the brownies Doc Reggie baked on Mitch's birthday. He closed his eyes. There. Everything backed off. But then Manny altered her moves. Her hands hit his chest. She bowed her spine and cool air hit his shaft as she lifted off. Brutal pleasure slammed into his groin, his balls tightened and nothing was going to stop the eruption that threatened to steal his mind.

Manny rode him quickly, balancing her weight between his chest and his cock. "You get so deep." The words gusted from her. Her heart double tapped her ribcage while her lungs labored under the actions of lifting and sinking onto his cock.

Rick lifted her, letting her drop onto his body. She shivered and bit her lips. Around his dick the slick channel pulsed with her orgasm. The trumpet of the Drakken swelled in his throat. He kicked back his head.

The instant he no longer focused on the exact pivot where their bodies became one, Manny struck his pectoral with sharp fangs, thanks to the partial shift. Rich and warm, the elixir of his blood slipped down her throat and the Drakken in her skin relished his taste. He went wild between her thighs. The roar that followed the savage trumpet filled the room. The scent of blood destroyed any inhibitions between them.

Manny sank her nails into his chest. The blood she drew stopped with a few licks of her tongue. She bounced up as Rick thrust from below. The penetration drove pain through her body. Manny tipped back her head, holding on with everything while he rode her from underneath. His lunges lifted them off the mattress. There would be bruises where his hands fastened tightly around her.

Orgasms swallowed her, waves breaking so quickly she never completely surfaced before the next took her breath, stole her sanity, bound her to the male under her with no chance of separation ever again. She let go. Trust flared white hot. Love smashed through her being with the last upward thrust. Their bodies locked together and spikes erupted the entire length of his cock. The force of them cut wedges into her pussy, digging deeper as the orgasm crested, slamming through her.

The plunge from flying so high took control. Manny let the darkness take her. The black swell dragged her under. Her Drakken went with her, unable to hang on. The last sight was Rick's face, eyes wide and Drakken bright, lips parted over a savage grimace. His shoulders bulged as he held her steady. The word *mine* surfaced in her failing consciousness. *Mine*.

***

Rick held her until the spikes withdrew. When she tipped over onto his chest he'd relished holding her close. Her cum mixed with blood created a chilly coating over his balls. He rolled her to her side, going with her. Once she was secure, he got out of bed. He staggered to the bathroom. A bath sounded good. He ran the tub full, added bath salts. He didn't have anything with a scent. He shrugged.

He went back to the bedroom and scooped her up in his arms. She weighed nothing. Awake she projected a fierce warrior vibe that set her apart. The only other person who ignored the back away sign was Trevor. The thought of the other mission tech made Rick bare his teeth again. The growl low in his chest caused Manny to mutter and frown in his arms.

"Shh." He stepped into the bath and found the built-in seat with his ass. He lowered her into the swirl of water. The jets he'd set to fizzle, nothing hard enough to pummel muscles. Manny stretched in his arms without waking. He leaned back in the seat, arms around her. "Pixie, did I pass the test?"

CHAPTER 27

In the rear-view mirror Mitch watched the car approach. He was on a long stretch of highway between towns in the foothills of north Georgia. The state line was coming up. The car roared past him. It was only then he saw the barest silhouette of a second car traveling behind with the lights out.

"We have company." The growl startled Gareth from his drowse. He leaned forward to peer out his mirror, his hand already reaching for the gun at his side.

"What's happening?" Spencer leaned forward then turned to look behind them. The car was too close. "They're gonna hit us."

"We should be so lucky," Mitch muttered.

"The lead guys?" Gareth pointed.

"Yeah." So far Mitch followed the car, but any moment that car might stop. The nearest exit was six miles ahead. His gaze sprinted around the road, checked the ditches, the lanes, oncoming traffic. There was none. Whoever this was knew what they were about. That meant trouble. "They're good as we are and we're alone. Call James." He had the infants and was just behind them. If they had any luck on their side, the pair of cars were on Mitch and crew alone.

"Trouble. Waiting on possible PIT and we'll be in the ditch." Gareth spoke softly, his attention on the car behind them.

"Wait a second," Spencer's voice chimed in from the back. Alarm empowered his words.

"I need you to sit back and be quiet." Mitch's tone didn't invite a response. "Both of you."

"Shit." James's expletive came over the line. "We'll keep an eye out."

"Get off the road, protect the assets." Gareth snapped the connection and pocketed the phone.

The car ahead slowed. In the dark, the red lights filled their vision, with wavelengths close to that they'd trained in *Below*. Their Drakkens sat up and focused. Their time was close. It was fight or die time. Gareth shrugged his shoulders, rolling them as the creature got ready to play.

"Are you good?" Mitch caught the impatient movement out of the corner of his eye.

"Ready." Gareth no sooner spoke than the predicted happened. The car ahead sped up, the trail car moved up to the back-quarter panel and turned hard into the SUV.

Mitch tried to hold onto the wheel, avoiding the ditch. With the tires skipped over loose gravel the top-heavy vehicle swayed. He fought speed and loss of traction, straightening the SUV into the right-hand lane. There was no exit in sight.

"Commander, whenever you're ready." Gareth's voice growled deeply with the Drakken's tone.

"Commander?" Spencer croaked from the backseat. Senoia kept silent.

The car struck, and this time Mitch had prepared. "We're going off the road." The ditch he'd avoided earlier flattened out. There was a catch fence, more to keep deer off the road than to stop a speeding vehicle. He held tight to the wheel, trying to keep all options open, and all unfriendlies in sight.

In the dark the headlights missed the deadfall in overgrown grass. The SUV hit it a glancing blow and that was all it took to tip. The heavy truck followed the rules of physics. Landing on its side it slid into the fence, where it stopped with a wheezing sigh.

Mitch hung in the seatbelt. Gareth freed himself and crawled over the seat back. He looked for the unfriendlies. Not seeing them, he used the techs in the backseat to step into the cargo area. Opening the door, gun back in his hand, he let the hydraulics lift the gate. Immediately the pfft of silenced lead filled the air. He moved out of the back and into the shadows on the roof side of the SUV. He kicked out of his unlaced boots, dropped his 9mm into one of the boot shafts and stripped.

The Drakken roared into the night. Only one passing car sailed by, showing no hesitation as the lead car now turned on standard police flashers after it rolled to a stop. Gareth's Drakken took to the air, distracting attention from the others stranded in the SUV. The lead vaporized against a shield of wind that spun silent before Gareth. On silent wings, he looped and dove to the damaged car. His small size made the maneuvers easy.

At the last minute he braked and turned his body around. Feet first he struck the driver. The impact was final, neck snapped against the door frame. Lifting on hard wingbeats he barely skimmed the ground to turn and attack the second passenger.

He heard more gunfire. None directed toward him. The lead car, phony police cruiser had the shooters. He took care of the second gunman. Going to his feet Gareth checked out the car. Both dead and no other riders. He craned his neck to check Mitch. The commander stood behind the SUV, using the bulletproof body to steady his aim as he returned fire at the decoy car. Before Gareth could engage, they sped away in the lead vehicle, turning off the lights. Gareth didn't waste a moment. He moved to the SUV and shoved it upright before shifting.

"You guys okay in there?" Mitch holstered his weapon and walked to the passenger side. Due to their serious after-market upgrades the SUV didn't have much of a scratch. No dints bent the door or frame. He moved to the window and looked inside.

Spencer stared back at him, eyes wide, pupils blown, hands over his solar plexus. "Gods balls, Gareth, he's been hit." Mitch feared the worst. There was a lot of blood in Spencer's hands, more of it spilled down his shirt, pooled in his lap.

Gareth joined him nearly dressed. "He'd gone, Mitch." Gareth tried though. He opened the door and stretched Spencer out. "The abdominal aorta's been severed." He looked back at his commander, there wasn't a damn thing they could do for him.

Mitch glanced over at the boy's sister. "You understand what Gareth just said?" The girl nodded. She hadn't spoken, hadn't uttered the first sound he could recall. Mitch shook his head. "He won't last much longer. If we were close to an emergency room with a staff of surgeons, he wouldn't survive." Again, she gave him a single nod, narrow chin up and down. Maybe a full inch, he figured. "I'll leave you to say good bye."

Gareth finished dressing and laced his boots. "Laurel went pro this time." He nodded his head at the dead pair. They stepped to the back of the SUV to give her space.

"Where the hell is he getting the money?" Mitch created his own crop circle in the high stalks. He kept pacing the same trek.

"Someone with deep pockets, that's for sure. These guys weren't cheap muscle. They're mercenaries, well trained and well provisioned." He finished the buttons on his cuffs. "Jake can find it. He's followed a thin web before." Gareth straightened with a deep sigh. "What about them?" He tipped his chin to the dead mercs.

"Any identification? Any obvious signs of cause of death?"

"No, sir. Broken neck, back." He shrugged. Gareth had been thorough. Professionals knew the score. They didn't carry anything into a job to create a trace.

"It'll be a mystery to GSP, there's nothing we can do. Get them into the car, don't leave a speck of anything."

"Sir." Gareth moved away.

Mitch turned back to the SUV in time to hear one clear sob. He sighed. Another complication to deal with. He hoped James made it home without incident.

***

James glanced behind them again. "I'm pretty sure we have a tail." He'd left the highway and was following the secondary road. He didn't think it was much of an improvement over streaking up the interstate highway. They'd passed through one town. The traffic signal lights on automatic yellow, blinking red on cross streets. Now the road dropped to a wide asphalt ribbon with fields like bookends to either side.

"Mitch warned us." Max rubbed his hands together, a nervous habit. "Can you lose them?" He scouted the road ahead. No answering glare of headlights. They were alone in the middle of nowhere.

"I wouldn't think twice, but with the infants?" He shrugged. James's hands tightened on the steering wheel.

We will be safe in your protection. The voice broke into the men's thoughts. *I am Kelby, my kin is Haydn. We are tougher than you think.*

"Was that one of the babies?" The disbelief in Trevor's question filled the truck. Any other instance his timing would elicit laughter. Tonight, there would be no chuckles.

"Nice to meet you, Kelby and Haydn." James told them. "I have a son, James. We call him BJ. He's a little older than you two. He is tough, as well."

Only one? We have met BJ. Inside the men's minds a foreign language flurried then stopped as abruptly as it started. *There is another voice with us. You do not hear him?*

They do not hear us often. There must be great need or closeness. BJ joined the conversation to clarify a couple of points. *I am BJ. James is my name, although they have always called me Baby James, after my father.*

We have no father.

I will give you mine, BJ assured them. *He is strong and teaches me many things. You have no mother and so you will have mine, as well.*

We thank you for reaching out to us now and before. Kelby answered for the boys. *I wondered if we would be together.*

I never doubted we'd meet, BJ assured them with quiet confidence. *The way may be rough before you get home.*

We are strong. Kelby asserted, satisfaction and contentment in his tone.

James didn't have time to respond. The road curved ahead, leaving them blind. The tail sped up and moved in close behind. If the car tapped him the truck would lose traction and they'd be an out of control sled, at least until they went off the road and into a ditch or field.

"I'm going to trust you." James checked the road ahead and floored the SUV. They'd practiced with the heavier weight and the loss of maneuverability. "Hold on."

"Who you trusting, James? Like not the kids, right? Cause they're babies and—"

James shook his head once to the right and followed to the left. Then all his concentration went into containing the truck and dodging the car determined to take them off the road. The engine answered his demand. The brawny roar cut through the night music. He pulled ahead of the car, taking them by surprise.

James drove into the dark curve, his eyes focused on every inch gained by the headlights. He whipped the truck through the S curves and took the center lane as the strip of road straightened. As soon as the land leveled and the lights behind him appeared he swept the SUV into a one-eighty. Now head to head he floored the truck again.

Driving toward the oncoming car, James held the wheel steady. “Ever play chicken?”

“Not with the babies,” Trevor gulped.

“Every chance I got.” Max chuckled. The sound was tight for the big man, the tone woven with his Drakken’s deeper nature.

“Ever lose?” James pressed his back against the seat, rested his head against the head rest behind it.

“Only once.”

CHAPTER 28

James didn't respond, every sense focused on the car in front of him. It slowed as he ploughed ahead. The car hesitated then rolled backward with increasing speed. "Not the smart way out of this," he forced through gritted teeth. He chased the car into the curves, watching as the driver lost control and the ass end of the car headed off the road. A back-end collision left the driver's side wedged in the tree line. The whine of spinning tires filled the night. James pulled up behind the car and braked gently to a stop.

Trevor climbed from the rear of the truck, Max joined him on the road. Guns out, they waited for movement from the car. When no one volunteered to get out, Max forced the invitation. "One at a time." The growl carried easily. At the crunch of metal and the crack of the tree trunk the night sounds ceased in the area a second time.

The passenger door opened. "Hey, Danny's hurt."

"He'll have to move slower." There was no flexibility in Max's reply. "Who are you?"

"Uh, we work for some doctor." The man stepped out of the car, keeping the dubious cover of the door between his body and two weapons.

"That wasn't the question I asked you. I don't have enough patience for this tonight. I'm tired and hungry and I want to go home." Max moved closer. He hoped the men wouldn't notice his barefoot state. The clothes would be a total loss, but in the boot of the SUV a go-bag with extras waited for an occasion like this one. "Danny, you're next. Get your ass outta that car."

"Told you he was injured."

"My response is I don't give a shit. Get him out of there or I'm shooting the stupid son of a bitch through the windshield." The Drakken hovered close, a tense spring coiled ready to explode and defend the youth in their SUV. A mere breath split Max between human and shift. Max paused a moment. "You know what you're dealing with." The standoff lasted six seconds. Max counted.

Danny pushed out beside the speaker, swaying, and holding his side. Max motioned them out from their shield. Danny nodded and leaned on his partner. There was no fooling Max. Danny moved well for someone purportedly injured. Both men looked in peak condition in the glare of the headlights. James turned on the twin spots and the brighter night turned to full-on day.

Trevor moved from the rear of the truck to the front, his bow up and ready. He stood in deep shadow. At the first furtive movement from Danny he drew back and sighted his arrow. Good thing. As soon as the injured mercenary cleared the door, both hands lifted, fists curled around the butts of two handguns.

Max reacted. The big blue Drakken took shape between the vehicles. The element of water his to call, the hot lead chilled, slowed and morphed as it struck his scales. Wings spread, Max snaked his head forward, taking Talker down with a slam, head to head.

Trevor took a breath and released it and the string at the same time. Max was so close to the shooter. The arrow flew true, striking the intended shoulder. Danny's arm collapsed and he reached for the arrow with the other hand. Both guns were now out of commission.

Max advanced, spread his wings to block further shots and trumpeted into Danny's face. The man dropped to the ground, hands out and empty. Trevor sprinted out of cover. He took the guns, checked both men for any other weapons and helped the least injured Talker to his feet. Danny he left on the ground. A little dew wouldn't hurt him.

"Who are you?" Trevor asked. He took hold of the arrow and wrenched it out of the soft tissue where it struck. He ignored the yelp and the curses, waiting patiently for them to die down.

"Danny. We work for a doctor." He started upright when Max swung to look at him. A puff of condensed air blew over Danny and the man paled and shivered in the blast of cold. "It's a team effort."

"Tell me something I don't know." Trevor pulled a knife from the leather sheath at his waist.

"Hired by the guy, he paid up front. Gathered the team. We trained together for a month then he called us up a couple days ago. We've been tailing you."

"J? Think the commander wants to talk to this guy?" Trevor didn't take his attention from the man in front of him. A dangerous enemy is one wounded and cornered. The LEDs reflected a blue glare off the polished blade of his knife.

James watched from the driver's seat. There was no way he was leaving the boys alone. Besides, he liked to see the other teammates shift and set their individual talents into play. He called Mitch. "Hey, you were right. I have two in an unmarked sedan, slammed against the tree line in some little dark stretch of road in Podunkville."

"If they're capable of talking, we'll talk. Any way you can get them to the state line rest area? Should be deserted until the patrol goes through."

"Yes, sir. We'll make room." James put the phone in his lap. Mitch disconnected the call. "Tie them up and bring them in. We're going to make a rest stop ahead."

Trevor wasted no time. He zip-tied Danny, and tugged him to Max. Max herded him to the back of the SUV. They waited while Trevor woke the unconscious man and zip-tied him. Trevor helped him to his feet and guided him over to the patient gathering. James lifted the trunk and grabbed the go-bag for Max. Trevor urged them into the back of the truck, head to feet and then zipped their wrists to the opposite ankles.

Max dressed out of sight, retrieved his boots and the ripped clothing. He scouted a moment for his gun. When he'd changed the clothing went everywhere. He tucked it into the bag and put it in the floor at his feet. "I'm going to have to talk to Mitch about the holster thing."

"You want elastic?"

"We need something." The hatch slammed and halted the conversation. Max watched as Trevor regained his seat between the infants. He nodded and James put the truck in reverse and hit the road. He was several exits away from the way-point Mitch chose. The run was silent. They pulled into the shadows of the rest area, parked beside Mitch's vehicle. Max got out and opened the hatch to introduce their cargo.

***

"Have you checked your messages?" Rick held the phone in his hand. It was the morning after an incredible night. They'd both survived and discovered much about each other. With the bond between them firmly set, the morning started out on a different note than any before. He hadn't planned on calling it a honeymoon, but it seemed to have worked to solidify the claim between the Drakken. His heart filled with love that he'd gotten used to telling about Manny every hour.

"No. What's up?" Manny got up from the table and crossed the kitchen to where she'd plugged in her phone to charge. She walked close enough to bump him with her hip, covered by a satiny robe and nothing else.

"Mitch is calling us home. There've been some major developments." Rick got to his feet. "Guess the honeymoon is over." He moved to her side and took her in his arms. Manny turned to face him in time to get his kiss. Their lips clung and Manny turned her body to fully press her front against his. Rick groaned as the now familiar nudge of desire sent blood coursing to his dick.

"No time." Manny smiled and broke the kiss. She locked gazes with him. "You know it's important." She kissed him a quick peck. "Honeymoon? You don't think I'm not going to make you marry me and take me on a real honeymoon?"

"You'll get your bells and whistles." He pulled her tight. "I love you with all my being, Pixie. But the commander has no sense of timing." Rick released her, taking a step back. "Okay. We don't have much to pack and we're only three hours from home."

Dressed in black leather, they left the house minutes later. The rutted trail took less time to navigate in the daylight. The sun was high and the ride took no time. They pulled into Mitch's driveway, riding up to what the team had started calling the Compound. With the bikes kicked on the stands, Manny released her chin strap and tugged the helmet off her head. She glanced at the door as it opened. Rick behind her replayed her motions.

"Have a good night?" Trevor stood on the porch.

"Why, you?" She wondered which of the Trevor's came to

meet them. Manny carried the helmet in one hand, the other tucked the keys into her pocket.

"Because you love me best." Trevor would always needle her. The old Trevor reappeared, the bratty younger brother she'd never had. Rick stepped up behind her, towering over Trevor.

Manny's lips crooked as she watched his throat work a swallow. *Intimidation did work on the irrepressible. Good to know.* "We're here to check in. The phones were on charge when the call came out."

"Aww, we took care of everything." Trevor stepped back into the entry, waved them in and closed the door behind them. "Everyone's in the COMM center."

"This is my home, I'll have you remember." Carrying a crowded tray, Regina joined them from the kitchen.

"Sorry, Doctor Regina." Trevor didn't look sorry. "Everyone seems to be using the term."

"Copycat," Rick shot over his shoulder. He moved to Regina, bleeding southern charm and chivalry. "Gimme that. I assume it's going down the hall?" He tipped his head and she nodded.

"Thank you, Rick." Regina smiled at him. She couldn't help but notice the tooth-produced bruises on his neck. She'd bet next month's paycheck he had others not so visible and so did Manuela. "Manny, I need you a moment." Without waiting for acknowledgement, she turned and walked back into the kitchen.

Manny watched the guys go. Rick speaking to Trevor in a soft tone, too soft for her Drakken to hear. Damn it all. Again with the interrogation? She so wanted to follow them. This was of import to her as well. She was part of that team, she'd participated in the missions last night and there was a debrief waiting on her. She turned to the kitchen. If she'd learned nothing else, it was that Regina had the ear of her boss and Manny would do everything she could to stay on the good side.

Putting it off would only convince Regina there was something to this. She took a deep breath and moved across the foyer and into the kitchen. She stopped at the door. Tracy was there with the three infants. "How are things?"

Manny watched Regina stir a crock pot the size of a farmhouse sink. The scent filled the kitchen and her stomach growled. "Fine." She glanced at the trio of infants. They were in infant carriers clustered together on the top of the table. “Everyone okay?”

“A little tired from all the excitement last night, but they’re doing well.” Tracy all but chirruped from her seat beside them.

“Yeah, about that. I need to debrief.” Manny pointed down the hallway. Happy for the easy escape.

“And then I want a debrief.” Regina replaced the lid with a glass clatter and turned to face her reluctant patient.

“No reason, we’re good. Promise, Doctor.”

“I saw evidence.” Regina nodded her head. “You’ve been a little less than gentle with each other.”

“You know we heal immediately. Something about the sex, having it.” Manny *just* managed to keep the scold out of her voice. She continued to back away from the kitchen and all the domestication going on inside of it. “If I have something come up I’ll head your way.” She made her escape with a half wave and a last glance at the carriers.

CHAPTER 29

Manny had to pause in the hallway before she entered the conference room where Mitch gathered the team. She took several breaths, held them, released them in time with her slowing heart beats. She straightened her shoulders, steeled her spine, and walked into the room with her usual confidence.

She leaned against the wall, tuning in with interest to the ongoing conversation. Her gaze rested on two men strapped hand and foot. Their expressions guarded, they didn't look up as Mitch continued.

"Laurel thought to best us again. As far as we can ascertain, these are the only two remaining minions. Unfortunately, their cohorts met with an accident of gravity. We have all the information from both labs, according to the surviving doctor."

Manny's questioning gaze met Rick's. He gave a one shoulder shrug. "I'll tell you later."

"The infants are well and thriving, as most of you noted on arrival." Mitch cut his gaze to Manny, acknowledging her tardiness. "They'll be adopted officially." He paused. "Now we have two issues that need to be dealt with before we can go after the mad scientist himself. He's without his hired hands. He's lost the Drakken infants and, unless he takes notes by hand, all of his precious research." With a deep sigh, he nodded his head toward the bound men on the floor. "And these two gentlemen for hire who have stumbled into their worst nightmare."

Hands punched the air. Too many for him to answer. Mitch looked around at his team and crossed his arms over his chest. With this mixture, he wondered what the first question would be.

"Go clockwise." His only directive.

"It's obvious we can't turn them over to law enforcement." Max pointed to the pair. "There's been way too much exposure."

"Mind wipe?" Gareth offered with a shrug. "That seems less than final and we can take them into the country and release them." A few chuckles met his deadpan comment. The situation was anything but comical.

Rick shrugged and passed.

James added his comment. "They knew the odds when they signed the bottom line. They were hired to take us out. They almost made it with Mitch, killed the girl's brother and attacked infants. They more than earned their sentencing." No one assembled exhibited surprise. By the time he stopped speaking, the Drakken surfaced from inside James, adding his power and conviction. Both put the infants first, protection of the species.

Derryck kept silent. He'd been on duty at the Compound when everyone made it home around dawn. He'd helped sort everyone on arrival, escorting the silently weeping girl to her temporary room. The sight of her in person gut-punched him. Her tears woke the Drakken inside. The big guy took notice of the anguished woman, a tightly focused and sexual notice. Anyone who'd caused her pain and the waves of agony radiating from her deserved to meet his savior. The beast inside wanted to take away the pain in exchange for all the pleasure he could mete out.

"We'll table that for now. I'll make a call, see what Greg has to say about it." He nodded at the team. "Anyone have anything else to contribute? Any issues to get off your chest?" No one spoke. "Dismissed."

"Good thing, Regina has the house full of good smells and my empty belly's growling." Trevor pushed his seat back under the table and headed past Mitch. Gareth and James took places beside the prisoners. Rick walked to Manny's side.

"Feels like we missed a couple chapters," he said softly as they left the room.

"I'm good with that." She took his hand, slowing his advance to the kitchen. "Hey, Regina's being nosy. She mentioned the marks we left on each other." Her gaze found the tell-tale on his throat. "Wants a check-up for both of us."

He smiled and tugged her hand. He wasn't sure if she'd give in and let him hold her. There were too many bodies still moving around. Behind them, Mitch and the others were still with the prisoners. Ahead of them, the bunch filled the kitchen and the noise level was rising.

Manny wanted the closeness and stepped into his hug. Rick's embrace seemed to make the day so much better even if it was still morning. She inhaled his warmth, wrapped her arms around him, and leaned her head against his chest. Manny absorbed his strength and appreciated his patience. Her psyche, still raw from wounds ripped open after too long, hurt. With the quickness of transformation on too many levels and life intruding, she hadn't had much time to internalize everything life-changing that happened in the last twenty-four hours. Thirty-six hours? Manny lost track.

Pixie, you okay? Rick didn't speak aloud. He kept his arms around her.

I will be. I need time. This is a lot of adjustment.

I'll see what I can do to buy it. Rick kissed the top of her head then pulled back to dislodge a silky hair from his lips.

What did I miss? Manny held still in his arms.

"Not much. We lost the IT twin to Laurel's mercenaries." Rick kept his voice down. "It couldn't be helped. Even if we'd been there he'd have bled out from the random shooting."

"Gods balls." Manny propped her chin on his shoulder. "How is the sister holding up?"

"No one has said. She's been in her room. I think Derryck is checking on her. He wasn't on mission last night, so she doesn't see him as a threat or as part of the group and activity that murdered her brother."

"What a fuck-up." Manny sighed her whisper against his neck. *We'll see this through*. She didn't want to appear as if she were shirking her duties. Rick said they couldn't have saved the young man. They'd been absent

Of course, Pixie. We're part of the team. Rick loosened his arms. "You ready to grab a bite?" He looked toward the kitchen. "If they leave any for us."

Regina had a few more pointed questions and at least a partial exam for them to suffer through.

An hour later in Regina's office, Manny followed the doctor's directions. Regina analyzed her from head to toe, took her blood, swabbed her mouth bottled the swab for testing and performed a pelvic exam. Rick went through the same basics, escaping the feet in stirrups.

"You're both better than I'd worried you'd be when we met again." Regina nodded at them. Rick was buttoning his shirt when she told them the results. "I sent everything to Ben since he's keeping comprehensive records. You both haven't healed from your latest exploits. That concerns me." She looked up from the tablet in her hand. "I wonder if the bond has set. Maybe the sex isn't as healing as it should be?"

"I told you." Manny shrugged into her jacket. "We've been on short sleep and rations. We'll catch up with the Drakken soon enough." She struggled to keep her tone level and relaxed. "Hell, Regina, it's a few bruises."

"Better you let me check." Regina smiled at her reluctant patients, knowing their medical history and imagining what happened earlier, more than once, if the bruises that lingered behind told her truth. "I know how things are now, so I can update your medical files and then put them away until you begin a family." She turned to her tablet and typed in a few sentences.

"Family?" Manny paled and swallowed as soon as the word slipped out. Her gaze locked onto Rick's. He showed the same surprise. It wasn't like they could use condoms. Well, after the first time. The spikes would render them useless and likely a hazard to then be removed by the lovely doctor. No way would she go there.

"Like the little boys in the living room?" Regina nodded and then closed the files on the screen. "You remember them, right?" She chuckled at seeing them stare into each other's eyes. That wasn't exactly the loving look of most committed relationships. An adorable infant chirp told her at least one of the boys was awake. She had nursery duty until the team returned. Tracy and James had left earlier to reinforce the inventory at their new home for triplets.

Regina left Manny and Rick alone in the room. They finished dressing, exchanged glances that gradually warmed until heat filled them. Manny knew her face flushed. The thoughts she contemplated about Rick aroused her. Her nipples peaked, her pussy grew damp and the channel that snugged his cock tightened with want.

"Um, you want to, maybe, take a walk?" Rick stomped his heel into the boot. He didn't bother lacing them. He wouldn't be in them much longer.

"Sure." Manny licked her lips. A new nervous habit maybe? She joined him at the door. He held it for her. They slipped past the archway into the living room. Regina had plenty of help with the infants. Both Trevor and Mike were at hand.

Rick held the front door open and they slipped out into the night. As if the winter refused to let go, though the ground retained the heat of the day, the air chilled. The result was fog, thick and thin in layers and moving in damp undulations around them as they walked away from the lights and building.

They didn't go far. Mitch's house only sat on five acres. That meant if they took another dive as Drakkens, the house would likely hear the trumpets of their flying forms. It couldn't be helped. They stopped as one, a silent accord. Their clothes dropped around their feet and they backed away from each other.

In moments, they shed the bipedal human form and stretched wings in silence before leaping into the humid chill air. Their wingbeats cleared the fog, rolling the layers into huge vortices. They cleared the fog bank, wings carrying them higher where the air thinned and grew cold. The stars sparkled this high. The moon, a bright white crescent, gilded their wings silver.

Manny watched Rick circle lazily above her. The mere sight of the great orange Drakken stoked the fire already burning deep inside. She hungered, not just as a woman, a female, but as a primal entity that needed him to assuage the inferno threatening to consume her. She drew in patience she didn't know she possessed. Her wings kept her in step with him. Slow circles took them ever higher into the night.

CHAPTER 30

Rick kept his eye on her, his ears tuned to her wings slicing through the night air. Sensual, supple, she danced on currents he was too heavy to use. The dark wine color of her scales hid her lighter shaded underbelly from the ground. The scent she perfumed the air with made him snap his jaws for the smallest effervescence.

He wondered why she shadowed him. Before, she'd taken control and he'd enjoyed giving her that freedom. His thoughts whirled in chaos. He'd not noticed how high they'd gotten. Manny moved under him, her wings matching his, beat for beat. She lunged ahead and he called out to her. Not the trumpet of lovers, of conquers, but a soft drone to question her intent.

Manny rose before him, took a second to flick her tail and then shot up in front of him. If Rick hadn't slowed, his nose would have caught the riff of fins along her spine. He hovered then raced behind her.

Mine.

One word, that's all she sent to him. One word that slammed into his chest and caused the double beats to halt then resume harder, faster. His mind filled with his answer. *Mine*. He caught her, twined his neck around hers. He moved around her, lined their bodies, and held her hips with his back feet as his dick found the entrance lushly prepared for him. He slid in deep, through slick muscles forced to accept every inch of him. He clasped her body with all four legs and pinned her wings.

They hesitated in the frantic climb for mere moments. Then gravity reached out for them with a greedy grasp. They rolled and headed for the surface of earth, head first, their bodies locked together in an intimate clasp.

Manny hummed before she struck Rick's neck close to his wing. His blood rushed hot over her tongue and immediately she licked the piercings closed. She closed her eyes, knowing the moment they had to separate and glide into the thinner air again. Her body shook with reaction, the way she did in human form when an orgasm possessed her. She arched her body, caught the wind, and moved high without hesitation. She wanted another one, more than one. She wanted those spikes to pierce her most tender flesh, marking her with blood and cum, a heady perfume.

Rick pulled her close, moved deeper inside the silken glove of her body, the head of his dick swelled and stretched the tight channel. She squeezed him with internal strength. The loss of even meager blood flow made him light-headed. They parted and he took off behind her. They chased beyond the very oxygen they needed to breathe. Clasped together in another freefall, he claimed her. Her blood lit his taste buds, her body took his deep inside.

There. Spikes pierced her, grabbed at slick flesh, biting deep in tender tissues. She opened her mouth wide, a silent clarion call as the orgasm exploded through her. The very wave of intense desire burned through her nerves, established new pathways. Her mind locked up as pleasure battled with pain. She hung in his hold, trusting Rick with her very life.

Rick pulled them from the spiral, his wings strong enough to support them both. He rose in the night, lazy spirals repeated as the moon measured the night with a slow tip. Long, hard pulsations ran from balls to the head of his dick, filling her with cum, mixing with her blood. He held her tight, a miracle in several ways. They'd broken through her defenses, found a haven between them to inhabit.

He licked her neck again. She'd stopped bleeding there. Inside of her, seated deep, he flexed and the fresh scent of her blood stirred things deep inside of him. Primitive feelings rose. The Drakken's nature emancipated. He couldn't help the primal trumpet. A male embedded in his female. Her blood coating his dick with their combined pheromones scenting the entire night as they claimed each other.

This was life. This was comfort, desire, ecstasy beyond all

thought. This was love.

Manny stirred in his hold. He needed to get them to ground. The spikes withdrew and he tugged his dick from her slickened depths. He kept hold of her until she roused enough to spread her wings. The movement was reluctant.

Are you okay?

I'm a little dizzy, but I feel wonderful. Manny chuckled. *I feel yours. I feel loved.*

Rick's chest puffed and the Drakken curled his neck, preening for her. He wanted her desire, her love. He kept pace with her, followed her to the ground and shifted on the landing the way he'd seen her accomplish the task. His weight carried him to his knees, but he didn't stay down long.

Manny waited for him. A beautiful smile relaxed her every feature. She would never be more beautiful than at this moment. He went to his knees before her, wrapped his arms around her waist and locked them behind her.

"I give you my heart, my soul, my body and spirit."

"I love you with all that I am." Manny ran her fingers through his damp hair. There was no shame, even though her fingers trembled.

***

"I'll leave them to you then. Pick up?" Mitch nodded, fist tight on the phone. Greg answered and they hung up. "A car will be here in an hour." He hadn't mentioned the children to his cousin. They would remain with the Brotherhood. That would remain non-negotiable. About Laurel though, there'd been something in Greg's voice. Some nuance Mitch didn't like.

Was Greg playing them? Had he wanted to keep Laurel from falling into their hands? What the hells was Greg up to? Mitch stared into space, his mind whirling with confusion that bordered on anger. Was Greg betraying them? He'd seemed legit, the man was family, still...

He'd heard several things he needed to investigate. Out of the mouths of babes. Well, the minds of infants, Mitch corrected himself, switching mental gears. He'd look into Greg later, cousin to cousin.

Jake was already getting records together for the boy's births, registering them with the county and state with names, and social security numbers applied for. He hadn't known how much having a baby entailed. Jake piggy backed Haydn and Kelby on BJ's birth, giving them triplet status. The certificates of live birth were signed by Ben Dugan.

James sat across from him. He and Tracy had agreed to take the other babies. The trio would grow up together. Mitch had to admire him. The man was virtually his second in command. He couldn't ask for a better one. In the field James was clear-headed, calm in an emergency and clever enough to think on the run. "You're sure there's another one out there?" Mitch hadn't taken the news well when James delivered it. "Some person who can communicate with the infants beyond BJ?"

"He was sure, and sure as well about the age of this other Drakken."

"We know this unknown can read minds from far away. He's been privy to every move we've made."

"That's exactly the conclusion I reached."

"Our mole?"

James shrugged at Mitch's question. "Makes sense. He's been outside looking in through each of us. He was in BJ's head before birth. He's slipped through our defenses many times. He's reported back to the mad scientist."

"How can we find him?" Mitch thought about the hours he'd examined John Moody's file, his background, his security links, and mental abilities, thinking he was the one betraying them at every turn. Yet under intense scrutiny Mitch had never discovered any subversive act.

"I think the kids are the best avenue. They can sense his 'voice' in their minds. Kelby and Haydn know his signature. BJ is older, but..." James shrugged, but the idea of his child affected or influenced by another older mind angered him beyond rationality.

"Yes." Mitch nodded. They'd lost Tracy, put the baby in danger. BJ had had to rely on his Drakken abilities to remain undetected to escape kidnappers. He'd suffered the separation better than his father had, but he'd suffered. "I don't see another way, honestly. We need to find this person."

"I'll work with them and see what I can find out."

"You and Tracy ready for so many demands?"

"Taking care of that this evening." James smiled.

***

Mitch checked his phone. Set on silent, the strong vibration moved the unit on his desk blotter. The crowd was gone, the house silent. He was in his office sorting through the information Jake sent over as part of the search for the mad scientist. Mitch was sure this time he'd catch the bastard and bring him down. He wasn't sure what a face-to-face would do to his tight control. Laurel had infected Regina without her knowledge and then buried them all in the underground lab not so affectionately known as *Below*.

That must be it. He leaned forward, the phone cradled in his hands as he used the app to pinpoint the address Jake just sent his way. The boy needed a realtor's license. He was getting well versed in digging up his "dead spots". This time the house rental went through several shell companies before Jake found the last hand on the lease, Doctor Emerson Laurel. Mitch called him.

"I'm sure it's him. The lease agreement has his signature. It's not like I don't have several others to compare it to, seriously Mitch." Jake leaned forward into the laptop's camera. "It's his house. I can watch it by borrowing time on the satellite, but I'm sure."

"Okay, I'll get a team together."

"Thanks, boss." Jake broke the connection.

Wasting no time, Mitch called in the team he'd need to get to the mad scientist. The hell with Greg and his wait and see what turns up. He'd take the bastard down by himself. He leaned back in his chair, looking out the dark window into the night, waiting for the acknowledgment he knew would come.

CHAPTER 31

Laurel had only himself to blame. He remained confused though. He hired the best money could buy. He'd planned for every contingency, or so he'd thought. He should have made them door guards for the nursery. The phone numbers for them remained unanswered where he'd previously left messages. There had been two on the news, a car accident. Both men died in the crash. Laurel didn't think it was an accident.

He'd buried his home in a bedroom suburb of Atlanta. Yes, the trek into and out of the busy city wore on him, time better spent on his plans for the lab rats. His paid muscle? There were four left. No communication. No updates on the infants. He snarled and drew back his hand to throw the phone against the wall. He caught himself. He'd been down before. It exhausted him, but he had the resources to start over. The blood samples, the core DNA samples, even the original tissue samples he kept safe in cryogenic storage in his basement. Infants took nine months to incubate. In less than a year he'd be back at this point. His backers would be patient, he was sure. He had assurances from on high his research and proof were worth the time. *I think I'll let them be in charge of hiring a team to work with. It hasn't helped me much in the past to hire outside my experience.* He snorted. *They'll send me half trained monkeys to assist.*

He didn't want to be within range of Mitch and his trained team. Maybe this time not within the United States. He'd go away to the Caribbean. Perhaps France, he hadn't visited the country for almost a decade.

He put the phone in his pocket, mind engaged in plans.

"This should be an easy grab. I want his ass back here in cuffs. I don't care if he's bleeding as long as he doesn't bleed out." Mitch paced before the three men he'd picked for the snatch.

"We know this intel is bullet proof?" Max asked, his gaze following every agitated step Mitch took. They'd been recalled just hours after dismissal. They were ready to go, anytime, anywhere.

"It is." Mitch didn't say anything more. He'd tried to call Greg but had gotten a secretary who had no clue of the general's whereabouts. A second call sent him to voice mail. A third simply rang until Mitch hung up in disgust. Had the mole they hadn't identified leaked information to the general?

"Wheels up, boys. You know what to do."

"Sir." They left the office and Mitch paced another round before taking his seat. He had a few hours to kill before the team reached the north Atlanta suburb. He picked up the phone to call Greg, again.

"Dr. Laurel, don't make any sudden moves." Laurel didn't react as though he'd heard the statement. He continued down the hallway. "Dr. Emerson Laurel, halt." Gareth's glance slammed into Max's gaze. He tightened his finger on the trigger. The report was softened by the suppressor on the muzzle.

Wood exploded into splinters, peppering his face with projectiles. Laurel covered his head with his arms and dodged around the door jamb.

"Now that I have your attention..."

"Who the hell— Never mind. I know exactly who you are," the mad scientist growled.

Gareth clenched his jaw to keep the shiver of memory from slipping free. He knew that voice from dreams, from hated memories steeped in madness and blood. A bogey man that haunted his subconscious. Max put his hand on Gareth's arm. It steadied him. He and his brothers had survived hell.

"Step this way, Doctor. You're coming with us."

"I think not, my boy."

Gareth snorted at the condescension in his voice. Laurel had always seen them as lab rats, no more, no less. "There isn't a choice. You'll come with us under your own steam or I will happily shoot you and haul your bleeding carcass back to end all of our nightmares."

"That's harsh."

"Laurel, step out." Gareth took half a step to his left, bringing the doctor back into sight. He lifted his weapon again, focused along the barrel, saw the laser lock onto Laurel's forehead. "Your choice of only two." Behind the taut scenario playing out, the back door crashed open. Gareth nearly pulled the trigger.

Masked men in green pixilated jungle fatigues rushed in. Three took stance behind Laurel. Gareth faced three AR-15 carbines. Each can hold 30 rounds. He had fifteen rounds, total. He was severely under armed for this face-to-face. There were more outside the back door. Gareth saw them take up guard. Between them a figure pushed through. "Stand down."

It was another voice in command of his past. Gareth had no emotional attachment to this man. Mitch would be curious about the change of plans. His cousin, the general, calmly moved up behind Laurel, took out metal cuffs and linked his hands behind him. Each crisp click of the bracelets sounded loud in the standoff.

"You can't arrest me, I've done nothing wrong."

"This isn't an arrest, Dr. Emerson Laurel. I'm not the police or the local sheriff. You'll be taken someplace more secure than Mitch's Compound," General Greg Dolca assured him.

Max spoke into the COMM set attached to his shoulder. He kept his attention on the action happening in front of him. Derryck waited in the SUV, sitting in the driver's seat. Mitch needed to know this ASAP. Derryck could listen to the mic and report.

Commander, there is a problem.

"Talk." Mitch recognized the mental touch of Derryck. Something was going wrong and quickly.

The general is here. He's taken Laurel. Derryck waited for the sonic mind scramble when Mitch lost his marbles. There was dead silence along the mental link. Somehow he thought that was more frightening.

"Sir, I don't have permission to allow you to take this man." Gareth tried to talk General Greg Dolca out of taking their quarry.

"Son, we met once. I allowed your little misfit team to continue as civilians. I need you to stand down and allow me to take possession of this asset."

Wrong choice of word. Laurel was anything but an asset. Gareth raised his weapon again. Too many safeties clicked off to count. Gareth took a deep breath. Never blinking, he stared at the general down the short barrel he'd had aimed at Laurel a moment ago. He'd be the first to die. The bullet in Gareth's gun was a higher caliber than the .227s pointed at him. The general didn't flinch, simply held his ground, his silence, and the upper hand.

Gareth could tell Dolca and Mitch came from the same genetic roots, a stubborn and hard to kill thorny vine, for sure. If Gareth moved wrong, he had no doubt the strike force would shoot him. He'd survive, he was sure. It would hurt like hell until then. He'd have to move outside to shift, even the smallest Drakken needed room. If Mitch gave the order, he'd bleed, but the general and the mad scientist would die this night.

He lowered the tip of the gun. Mitch knew what was happening. A fiery whip lashed through every operative's mind then eased away. Gareth held his stance, waiting for something he didn't know but hoped he'd recognize it when it happened. The house accumulated silence. A double buzz crossed the room with impatient insistence.

Dolca frowned and pulled a phone from his pocket. After a glance at the screen, Dolca let his frown move into a scowl. "Get him out of here." The general commanded his men. One stepped forward and all of them ignored the sputters from Laurel. They double-timed the mad scientist out the back door. One man kept Gareth in his steady sight as Dolca answered the call.

He didn't speak, not even to say hello and with Gareth's enhanced hearing, Mitch wasn't at all happy with his cousin. The bark of his voice, the rapid-fire questions, and the way Dolca winced amused him. Gareth holstered his weapon.

"We gotta go." Max nodded behind him, his dark gaze fixed on the general and remaining soldier. "Mitch wants us clear of this mess on the double."

Gareth tipped a sarcastic salute to the men. Taking his time, he turned and closed the front door behind them. They jogged to Derryck in the truck and jumped in. The engine was already running and the transmission in drive. Max took the back seat and Gareth buckled his belt while Derryck hit the gas and moved them away from the house and off the grounds.

He wove quickly into traffic. Random right and left turns assured Derryck there were no tails. He moved to the highway and headed north. They'd be home in a few hours. Mitch's tone told them he was unhappy that he'd lost this battle and that Laurel went with the victor this round.

Derryck settled in to the drive. The white lines flashed past the wheels as he drove into the night. He hadn't had time to talk with Senoia Knyght, and something told him they needed to do exactly that.

***

Yoseph Magellian cringed. An hour ago he'd had two choices. One to remain with Laurel, as he had since his modification by the original formula. He'd undergone the shifting process and Laurel had hidden him deep into the shadows. He'd been a mole and spy for months. When he'd discovered the plan to use human breeders for the next-gen project he'd felt disquiet. Still, he'd followed Laurel faithfully.

Yoseph remained Laurel's right-hand man, and he'd tracked the remnants of the experiment that happened in the underground lab for Laurel, finding them easily every time. He'd been close when Mitch mentioned to General Greg Dolca he had a mole. Yoseph knew better, but he'd enjoyed the chase-your-tail sport of his quarry. Mitch nearly caught him several times. He'd been close when they'd kidnapped Tracy.

Laurel made him back off. Now, look. The scientist had been arrested by the same people who'd financed the project. That last mental voice shut off mid-word. Yoseph believed the good doctor was dead. The military machine had many faces and deep secrets. Yoseph thought about the situation for a while. He had the feeling time was running out for him.

Choices? The only one remaining he wanted to consider was placing himself at the Drakken Brotherhood's mercy.

He'd never been a fighter. He'd turned to bookish studies and avoided physical contact most of his life. What could he offer them to keep him out of the hands of the government? He paced the little room, his hands clasped behind his back. It would have to come from the children. He'd been aware of each of the boys at birth. Born without preconceptions, they were friends to him, a man they'd never met but accepted. Yoseph couldn't count the times he'd been a good guy, accepted in his truth. Maybe that was the answer. He'd be as the children. A decision made, he packed and prepared to meet his future.

CHAPTER 32

Mitch's hand with the phone arced from his ear to his thigh.

"What happened?" Regina asked. She'd known Greg would call.

"Capturing Doctor Emerson Laurel will no longer be a consideration." Mitch's words fell about the audience. The phone call had taken less than a full minute and still less time to absorb the unexpected news.

"They executed him." Gareth nodded with his answer. He looked around at the gathered brothers. "Well, guess we're working with the shadow side of our great nation full time."

A chorus of agreement filled the room. Mitch took Regina's hand in his. She'd suffered worse than he had. Hell, the Brotherhood suffered more. They were still working to patch up psyches destroyed by that perverted bastard. He looked around the room, seeing the team move closer to a seamless being as he watched them digest the news. To many of them he'd been the singular night terror they couldn't shake. He'd been the shadow at the edge of their gazes, the bogey-man who visited late at night.

He'd taken their humanity and twisted it with the creature of myth and legend that lived under their skin.

"You're worrying." Regina tugged him from the room as the round-robin of comments continued. It would take time before the truth sank in with them. They were finally rid of the anchor that weighed their spirits. "Are you okay?"

"I'm planning."

"There's a difference?" Regina knew him well.

Mitch took her into his arms. His heart swelled at the

straightforward way she moved close. "We just closed an open file, one most of us wondered if we'd ever solve. It's a little anticlimactic. Greg took him and executed him. The end."

"What happened to his assets?" Regina asked between the kisses she placed on his chest.

"If there were any others, I have a suspicion we'll know sooner than later."

Regina glanced up at him, her brow wrinkled and confusion filled her expression. "Huh?"

Mitch smiled, shook his head, and kissed her the way he'd wanted to for some time.

***

Rick pressed kisses to Manny's belly then turned and put his cheek against the smooth flesh. They would have children, not now and not for years. They had a lot of missions ahead. Their life together had just started, so they had plenty of time ahead of them.

"Exactly." Manny agreed. Shadowing his thoughts was easier and less of an intrusion and she enjoyed it. She liked learning the patterns of his thoughts, his reasoning behind decisions. She loved the way she was so important to him, how he put her first. He didn't treat her as weaker. She was his equal, as she needed to be.

"Let's go home." Rick got to his feet for the second time. They dressed and without a word to those inside the house, they left.

***

He's coming to see us. BJ took lead with the other Drakken young. He was the oldest, after all.

He's not a bad being. Kelby gave a mental shrug.

Haydn kept his silence. Not that he didn't care. Yoseph Magellian was a person of interest. He'd be patient. He believed there was a familial tie between them. He'd soon find out.

The End

Coming soon from GDB After Dark

This is an unedited special treat for Carol's readers!

Derryck
Drakken Brotherhood
Book 4

Chapter 1

The green Drakken folded his wings. His momentum carried him forward a step and he caught himself before going down on his knees. He was tired beyond belief, his body barely able to stay upright. He'd been "in country" now for eleven days. He'd been hunted, chased openly though the twisted limbs of jungle, shot. Twice. One bullet Regina was waiting impatiently to remove.

He staggered toward the black truck, his mind still cataloguing any and every threat around him.

"You look like shit." Max's voice boomed out as he approached the vehicle.

Derryck didn't acknowledge him. His gaze constantly adjusted from close to far, hunting with exhausted desperation in every shadow for the enemy. He was alive, and like a good marine he'd keep his mouth shut until debrief. A flash of light kissed a stygian shade. He stopped his forward motion and his breath hitched. He blinked dry eyes, pain tearing at every nerve in his body. He thought she'd been there. The reflection of light off her hair, the way the silky length shifted over her shoulders when she turned—

"Yo, Marine, get your ass in gear. We gotta bug!" Max's voice dropped. They weren't in the safest part of town. This night hook-up was a reluctant pick-up from Mitch.

Derryck blinked. It couldn't have been her. She was safe in the Compound. Safe. Under Mitch's roof. Alone. That was a kick in the gut. But it got his feet moving to the SUV. He needed to stop thinking about her. Obsessions were difficult to break.

He tossed his bag into the truck and pulled the robe from Moody's hand. He'd held it suspended for Derryck as soon as he landed. Derryck wrapped it around him, taking his seat and closing the door. The slam caused his wince, he closed his eyes against one more pressure change and let his head fall back against the rest.

He needed to stop thinking about her. He needed to do a lot of things but that wasn't going to cease. There was something about her, something about Senoia that interested his feral Drakken.

She belongs to me.

Derryck didn't answer the husky voice of his other half. He'd tamed that beast months ago. Kept the creature under hard wrap. The wild half of him bowed to his control.

She's mine. I want her.

Derryck ignored the voice. He tried. He was tired, exhaustion creeping ever closer to take his consciousness. His hold on the wild one slipped.

She's the only one for me. We need to claim her, make her ours. She's waiting for us, she understands.

Derryck let the voice ramble on, closed his eyes and caught a battle nap. He was in for a brutal debrief. The mission had been shit and that's not all he had to report.

***

"Just stack them up. I'll get them put away in a minute." Regina told Senoia over her shoulder. They'd finished eating dinner and clean up. Tracy brought the triplets over. That's how everyone referred to the infants now. They were all sitting up and mentally talkative as they learn language. Regina held the runt of the litter in her arms. Haydn might always be weaker of the three.

"How is the little guy doing?" Senoia walked over to the pair. Tracy was on the floor with the other two, BJ and Kelby were playing and laughing.

"He's... Haydn." Regina turned the baby over to the newly certified doctor. The only good thing to come out of Greg Dolca's seizure of Dr. Emerson Laurel. He'd pushed through a "favor" and Senoia passed her last hurdle. Now officially, with sheepskin waiting for the perfect frame, she'd become part of their family.

"Hello, little man." Senoia took the little one.

Hello.

"Are you ready to play?"

May we go outside?

Senoia glanced into his brown gaze and nodded. "Regina, I

think we'll walk around outside for a bit."

"Good idea. It's a beautiful evening." She started a late-night dinner. Mitch told her Derryck was due in late. He'd want something not MRE. She'd already cleaned his apartment, bought groceries, and restocked his fridge. Mitch mentioned earlier he'd had a rough trip.

Senoia took the infant through the back door. The yard was freshly cut, storm clouds that threatened earlier were shades on the horizon. She took her time wandering around the acreage. Placing the boy with his back to her chest she held him close.

"Both of us seem to be out of place." Senoia told him, placing a kiss on his dark hair.

This is our home.

"It is. It's just..." Senoia walked a bit further. Haydn a warm bundle in her arms as the sun sank toward the horizon. "I miss Spencer." She took a few steps and sighed. "I miss Derryck." She took a seat on a bench and turned him to face her. "I miss them both. Is that strange?"

There is the Drakken to consider. We are strong and wild. Full grown we are forbidale. His little voice hesitated over the work. He'd heard it but found it hard to repeat. Haydn let his eyes change, a ruffle of red fluttered under his baby soft flesh. More snake than dragon, the soft color faded.

"Formidable," Senoia filled in. "I understand that. Still..." She watched the sun give up and let the day go. Twilight took it's turn, bathing them in shades of purple and red.

You need to mourn.

Senoia nodded. "You might be right. Spencer has been gone for three months. I know they took care of everything. They're good people." She looked down at him. "You realized that before I did."

Haydn nodded and grasped a lock of her hair in his fist. His gentle tug made her smile. He mirrored her look, his smile hesitant. *You are so sad. There is more I can sense but don't know the words.*

"Take your pick." Senoia chuckled. "I'm confused, especially about the things Derryck makes me feel. I'm angry about Spencer. We were so close nothing seems in a hurry to fill the void in my heart and my mind."

People always say time. Haydn yawned and blinked those

wide eyes.

"You're right, little man. Time is supposed to heal every hurt." Senoia got to her feet, tucking the infant to her heart. "You are so smart for one so young."

***

The babies were home with James and Tracy for the night. She'd excused herself earlier, showered, and put on pjs. Her feet curled under her in the chair in her borrowed room. Her borrowed room. That broke her train of thought. Senoia attempted to read a medical article on her computer, new DNA studies. She looked around her. She needed her own place. She'd been in rentals and had no furniture. Just the clothes on her back and a few things she'd been given as hand-me-downs.

Like these pjs. She'd never pick the garish rose print on them. They were warm and comfortable though and she liked the softness against her skin. Nothing reflected her personality. Tears formed. A sniffle filled the silence of her room. She closed the computer and turned off the light. Enough of that. Tomorrow she'd look around for a place to call her own.

She punched the pillow. The house around her remained silent. As she drifted off to sleep she wondered if Derryck made it back safely home.

***

Derryck hauled his ass out of the chair before Mitch's desk. He'd turned over video footage and transcripts he'd gathered. He'd eaten. Maybe that was his mistake. He'd filled his belly on top of no sleep and monumental stress. His muscles were spaghetti, his brain oatmeal. He wondered where all that Drakken strength was now he could use it.

"Hit the sack. Things will look better tomorrow." Mitch's gruff voice interrupted the internal dialogue and started his feet moving. He left the office, walked through the darkened living room and into the room he borrowed for the night.

He slipped into the darkness, pulled off his clothes and opened his eyes long enough to find the large flat surface that didn't match level with the floor. His destination was right there. He stumbled to the edge, sat down and dragged his lower legs up. His head found the pillow and he was asleep in the middle of the next blink.

Senoia didn't move, didn't breathe. She'd been startled out of a deep sleep by something. She glanced around the room, seeing a shadow approach her bed. She didn't know who slipped into her bedroom in the middle of the night. Danger fed her adrenalin and every muscle tightened in response. The person didn't make a sound. The weight hit the mattress and she realized it was a male. The soft sough of a snore filled the air. He must be one of the Brotherhood. No one else would be in the Compound. She was safe Senoia reminded herself. Her body relaxed, the dream beckoned and she gave into the pull.

The man beside her eased and the resonance of his breathing soothed her back to sleep. She slipped into the dream as if there'd been no interruption.

***

Derryck woke suddenly. Heat soaked his front, another body moved against his and he tensed. Light gleamed behind his eyelids. Morning had arrived. He searched his memory of the night before finding it spotty at best. Max got him to Mitch's. Regina, bless her very soul, fed him. He couldn't remember what he'd eaten.

He'd debriefed. That clear thought brought a snarl of worry. Had he included everything when he'd spoken to Mitch last night. Or was the correct timing of the meeting early morning? He couldn't remember. He had to open his eyes and find out what and who cuddled against him. He remembered going down into the pillow, his arms crossed over his chest, his legs stretched out. He'd learned the tight position on naval vessels. The bunks were narrow.

His shoulders pressed against the bed. He'd rolled over at some time. His left arm lacked feeling. Derryck inhaled slowly. A fragrance filled his head with richness, mystery, feminine. His Drakken pushed at Derryck's control, surged forward. He quelled the beast and opened his eyes.

Darkness curtained his sight. Long strands of hair blocked his clear sight. He'd imagined seeing these same tresses last night. One mystery solved. He fisted his left hand and released it. The woman resting on it rolled on top of him. He clenched his teeth against the moan the moved produced.

Now her breasts plumped against his chest, her chin over his heart, her warm breath stirred the hair on his chest. He was naked. Not that he remembered taking all of his clothes off, but the nudge of her knee against his stiff cock told the story. Senoia slept hard in his arms. He hated to wake her and even his astute mind couldn't produce a way to shift her over and desert this situation without waking her.

Mitch
Drakken Brotherhood
Book 1

https://www.amazon.com/dp/B0145T6FIW

Chapter 1

Commander Mitchell "Mitch" Bolton stood at attention. He let nothing of his opinion show on his face or in his eyes. Inside he was a seething mass of anger, the kind of destructive anger he'd fought so long to contain and control.

"Yes, sir."

"I know you, Mitch. You don't like this." The general sighed and left the window where he'd been watching the antics of the new recruits on the parade ground.

"You're my oldest officer here. I trust your judgment. But this is bigger than either of us." When he took his seat the old leather covering the chair squeaked as the chair groaned with the added weight.

"I need eyes on the inside, a mind that knows what to look for and how to interpret the information." Clasping his hands together, the general missed nothing in his commander's stance.

"Yes, sir," Mitch repeated, hardly willing to accept orders that sounded as if they were generated from any one of a hundred science fiction novels or movies, for that matter. It was a story old as the military. It resulted from some overpaid brain wanting to help the defense fund by creating a super soldiers, maybe even robotic ones.

"Permission to speak freely." Even knowing they were alone, Mitch still hesitated making the request. The general wasn't going to like his two cents worth, but Mitch couldn't hold back.

"Granted." As soon as the softly spoken word left his mouth, he leaned back in his chair as Mitch leaned forward, planting both hands on the desk.

Teeth bared in a hard sneer, he looked at his commanding officer.

"You seriously believe this trial will go into effect? That somehow, through folklore interpreted by a woman and a serum from a recipe book printed on bark, it will turn men into organic berserkers?" Mitch's voice remained a low growl, as if he wanted no one to hear the unreality he clearly outlined. He pulled his hands back, taking a step away from the broad divide between them. Body aching to move, he stilled every nerve, watching silently, grasping for control. If he let it all out he'd likely be facing jail time. It was imperative he clamp down on that need for action, at least until he cooled down and agreed to this impossible mission.

He took a cautious step and then another, feeling the rage disperse though his feet. Calming, he slowed his pacing and took several deep breaths. It was an old trick he'd picked up long ago, letting the anger drain away. It usually worked.

"I'm supposed to handpick a team of men from these volunteers who are to go underground and live." He raised his hand before the general could speak. He wanted no misunderstandings between them about this ridiculous assignment. "These men, every one, agreed to give their all, all of them Special Forces across all branches of the military, from SEALs to Raiders." The Marines finally reinstated their Special Forces group, giving it the same title as before it had been disbanded. MARSOCs finest and probably its youngest had been offered to the visionary project. Shaking his head, Mitch turned around to make another pass in front of the desk. "They volunteered for extra hazardous duty.

"I don't have issue with that. They signed on to fight and die for their country, but we plan to inject them with an untried serum and expose them to light studies that will determine how effective all of these "witchcraft potions" are at creating the perfect soldier." He ran his hand through hair that was already in need of a cut.

"I've been through some crazy schemes, but this takes the cake. Are you trying to poison us? Is this something on which we need to be wasting money and time? Hell, the man-hours and power waste alone boggles the mind. You do realize how futuristic this sounds?" He stopped the pacing he hadn't realized was moving him around the office.

"I know something about science fiction and this would be a box office flop." Mitch turned to face the desk and the man sitting behind it.

"I know how it sounds. This comes from very high." Unable to define the statement, the general sighed. "It isn't a choice. Not for me or for you." He pushed the innocent looking file toward Mitch.

"Here are the guidelines for picking the specific soldiers we're looking to recruit. Make sure all of them are volunteers looking forward to this mission. There is an abridged mission outline, also included there." He rounded the desk, moving to Mitch's side. The general met Mitch's level gaze as he slid over the thick file. "All we can do is our best to make sure this comes out good for all."

"Super soldiers based on Viking Berserkers." Voice filled with disdain with the very idea, Mitch looked down at the expandable file on the desk. The minute he reached for it he'd gave up the fight. There was no use fighting it. If Greg thought this was the best place for him, he'd be there. But he wanted Greg, as family and as his commanding officer, to know how badly intuition had dogged him since he'd heard the first rumor. He'd dismissed it as another scheme with no chance of gaining credibility. Unfortunately, the rumors proved true. The shadow that warned him of danger filled his head, standing firmly entrenched.

"I trust you to follow orders. Keep in touch with this office." Greg offered his hand. "Be safe."

Mitch hesitated, staring at his cousin. He took the offered hand and clasped it firmly in his.

"I'll see you." Greg pulled him close. Both men looked over their shoulders at thirty years of aging fading away quickly.

When they parted, Mitch held the information to his side. With a nod, he turned on his heel and left the office. Stomach tight, Greg watched him go. If the family trait ran true, this would not end well. Yet he had no choice. There were whispers of the lead scientist using military funds to perfect the process he'd kept secret. Once it was through testing and the specifics proven using the government dime, it was rumored the serum and the specific light wavelength that activated it would go to the highest bidder.

Greg rubbed the back of his neck, strain in the muscles keeping it tight. He returned to watching the new recruits, his mind far away. While he'd been raised knowing the story of the family's unique genetic makeup, his uncle, Mitch's father, had kept the secret away from his family.

Their bodies carried a strain of DNA not present in most other humans. It allowed them to age gracefully, to keep their incredible mental acuity well past human norms. Their bodies rejected viruses and bacteria, so they were never sick. A movement below, close to the building, caught his gaze. Greg sighed, glancing down as he watched Mitch stride angrily to the parked car. He wanted to let his cousin in on the secrets. There had been so many times he'd wanted to let Mitch know as boys. He'd never managed to break the silence about the forbidden topic.

A fine soldier, Greg finally managed to get Mitch stationed under him on the base, after the first notices of this new mission spec crossed his desk. With a sigh, he turned to sit at the desk, the weight of his orders weighing heavily on his shoulders. When he understood what might happen, Mitch was the logical choice. It would mean that Mitch was walking into this blind to his nature, but that very nature would be the one thing that would keep him alive. Of that, Greg had no doubts.

Mitch already doubted the mission without even seeing the specs. When the full story of the trials was uncovered, either he'd go MIA or he'd buck every level of the mission hierarchy until he'd torn down the Pentagon. There were facets Greg doubted on this mission. Luck ran with him that the ones who'd chosen this task for him hadn't known he had an ace in Mitch Bolton.

The man was hell against anything but straight up soldiering, and it showed. He'd be a valuable asset.

Mitch jumped off the helicopter after he'd tossed his bag to the ground. He learned to travel light long ago. Dust puffed around his feet, sweet and choking as the whirling blades lifted it and he waved the chopper away. Letting the air settle around him, he shifted the backpack and shouldered the loaded sea bag. He took a moment to look around. Camouflaged by the clinging desert dust, the house was part of the wildness around it. Behind the house rose a butte, shading it for now. In the afternoon, the sun would clear the ridge and the house would be at the desert's hot mercy.

Across from the front door the desert rushed out like a carpet, every shade of brown from cream to umber wove together in an incredible display. In the distance rose a ridge, jagged and inhospitable looking. There was a line, crooked through the carpet, twin ruts that probably were a roadway. It led away into the distance, disappearing around the tail end of the ridgeback. A van waited by the front door. Must be someone leaving.

He moved to the door, pausing with his fist raised, and then simply reached for the knob. They had to be expecting him. And according to the specs of this base, they had eyes on him the moment he landed.

Turning easily, he smiled at the implication of well-attended maintenance. The living room was homey and stuck in the seventies a good decade, long gone. A head peered around the door to the kitchen, he assumed, as the scent of fresh baked bread filled the air, replacing the dust in his lungs.

"You're new here."

"Smells good." Mitch stepped forward with a nod, slowing his next step when a 9mm eased into view. "I see." Holding his hands out, he dropped the bag. Moving slowly, he reached into his pocket for the billfold-sized packet he'd need to pass the guard. He tossed the packet to the feet of the baker. Never losing sight of Mitch, the male moved the packet past him with a booted foot.

"Please, come into the kitchen." The invitation was slow to come, but warm as the gun disappeared as quickly as it had appeared and as quietly.

"Mind if I catch my bag?"

"Of course, you'll need it."

Mitch complied, stomach growling at the scent.

"Butter?"

"I'm sorry?" Mitch asked and then turned into the room. A plate had been set with a slice of steaming bread.

"Would you like any butter on it? We have honey and peanut butter if you'd prefer."

"Honey is fine." Mitch dropped the bag in a free corner and accepted the bread, now generously topped with honey. The first bite was heaven, lost in the heat, texture, and sweetness, He didn't remember eating the rest. Another slice appeared.

"I am supposed to be here, we have the right-umaddress?" While Mitch thoroughly enjoyed the treat, he wanted to make sure this was the actual base.

A chuckle stirred the air. "You are in the right place. It takes time to cycle personnel. They called ahead and there are folks who need a trip to town. We're waiting for them to come up and for their ride to get here. Then you load and down you go."

Mitch ate the second piece more slowly, enjoying every bite this time. That explained the van he'd seen outside. Their ride was here. He studied the team in the kitchen. The silent guard watched him closely without appearing obvious. The talkative one opened the oven and the smell of chocolate chip cookies surpassed the fresh hot bread.

"Tea or coffee?" He turned and asked Mitch.

"Coffee, black and hot." The talkative one of the pair poured the cup and brought it over to where Mitch had taken a seat at the table. The chrome and yellow Formica reminded him of his grandparent's house, of all things. Scarred by cups and plates slid across the surface, not to mention buffed by elbows, it was homey. Silence filled the ranch house. A soft purr of wind stroked the outside, giving only a whisper of sound.

Mitch's natural worry kicked in, goaded by the shadow of danger, a constant companion. His mind whirled with the past month as he sipped the strong brew. It had taken him that long to handpick the men who were to join him down here. They were to allow no women for their first run of serum and testing. Mitch didn't like it, hadn't grown any more fond of the mission, no matter how many times he'd read the file on the specifics. He'd swallowed his distaste and hoped for the best.

Every soldier, sailor, jarhead, guardie, and flyboy he'd picked should already be here, housed and getting adjusted to their specific world. Every amenity was included, meals, gym, pool. There was room down here for a basketball court. He hoped all were fine without sunlight. For the next twelve or so months, there would be little of that. His expected the stay would be no longer.

Mission parameters set out time lines for eighteen months, two years, and three years. Based on the success rate, there were added instructions for women once the males proved proficient to the purpose. He sighed. Why the fuck the military wanted berserker women he gave up trying to explain. There was no way he could make sense of that or condone it.

He snorted. Call him old fashioned or a chauvinistic throwback, Neanderthal even, he didn't think women needed to be front line fodder. With them rested the future of the world. He trusted they were strong and capable, resilient. Targets for enemy action? Not so much. He had to draw the line somewhere so he could lay down his head and sleep at night.

They were giving up many things to participate in the trial. Not family, the men had no families, no children, and no ties. The orders were explicit on that point. Mitch's gut clenched. There was a better than even chance they would not return from these tests. That remained unspoken. Added to that, these men were in their sexual prime and there were few women *Below*. The natives had already named their home, he'd found out from the chopper pilot.

He'd spent the night before with a woman he knew, but he wasn't attached to her. She'd been a good time, and he was just loose enough from the sexual Olympics that had lasted until he left her bed for the base. He'd dozed while waiting for the chopper, transportation from the last duty station to this one. A real nap, stretching out in a bunk, now his hunger had been sated, sounded like the best plan for the day. He had to report to the man leading the mission, or testing as the civilians would have it. Then he had two days to settle in, make sure the roster was complete, and all would begin the testing, as long as no shit had hit the fan in the time he'd been out of contact traveling. There was always the chance something had gone wrong. How could it not? Given the insane logic trail for this whole venture, he didn't doubt trouble brewing for an instant. He set the empty cup on the table, still lost in thought.

He had a planner of things the men would need to do to keep busy. Too much testosterone, if not bled off, screamed trouble. The only alternative was to fill their days with tasks and their nights with exhausted slumber.

A grumbling noise, subliminal, brought him from the woolgathering. He looked around, trying to place the source of the growl. His host didn't seem to notice the vibration. Mitch stood, grabbing his backpack, guessing it was his ride.

"Head down the hallway. The end closet is the door." Like that, he'd been dismissed from the kitchen. The warmth of the previous conversation drained away. He shouldered his sea bag and stepped into the doorway of a bedroom to clear the hallway. Good thing, the door opened and a woman's voice filled the house.

“Regina wanted me to get her some cheap stuff, but she works so hard. I think I’ll go to the boutique in town and get her some really good scented soaps and shampoo.” As full of life as the voice, the short curvy woman reflected every erg of that energy. She led the way from the elevator, a force of one, towing three very bemused males behind her. Mitch watched them down the hall, stepping to take his place, only to fall back when another woman left the elevator.

Tall and less curvy, she nodded as she passed him.

“I’m Amelia Jenkins, one of the bio techs.” “Commander Mitch Bolton.” Neither reached out to clasp hands. Amelia nodded again, turning to follow the group into the day. Mitch stepped into the elevator. The weight of his bag suddenly seemed too heavy to hold as the responsibilities on paper became flesh and blood.

https://www.amazon.com/dp/B0145T6FIW

James
Drakken Brotherhood
Book 2

https://www.amazon.com/dp/B01LY30BFP

Chapter 1

Tracy paced the floor, one hand raking through the tangled frizz of her blond hair, the other cradling her belly. She'd called Regina. She couldn't keep the secret any longer. The doctor and her best friend would know what to do, what advice to give.

Jimmy had awakened her this morning with a goodbye kiss. She'd smiled and yawned, pretending she still slept. He left happy and she'd gotten up. A hot shower later, she pulled a maternity dress over her head. The summer print that looked out of place in the middle of winter was comfortable, and she needed emotional support.

The knock on the door startled her out of her musings and pacing. She hurried over and opened the door. Seeing Regina's curious smile she broke into sobs and fell into her cold embrace.

"Honey, what is it? Let's get you inside, keep you warm." Regina pushed her into the house and closed winter out. In the mountains winter came early, but the men were still practicing together.

Regina was sure Mitch was looking carefully at mission orders to test his team, wanting to cherry pick the best one for the combined brotherhood.

"What's going on, Trace?" Regina dropped her coat on the foyer table and moved them into the living room, close to where flames crackled heat into the room. She loved watching the cheery warm fire. She pulled her friend down beside her on the couch and held her sweaty hands.

"I'm pregnant." Another round of sobs accompanied the confession.

Reggie smiled. "Yes, I know. I found out six months ago, when you told me." It was a dark time for Regina, and Tracy had tried to coax her back to happiness. "Calm down and tell me what happened? You're starting to worry me." She slid back, nestling into the cushions. “It isn’t that stubborn husband of yours, is it? I can call Mitch and he’ll beat the snot out of him in the ring today.”

Tracy smiled, sniffled and shook her head. “Not Jimmy, exactly.” She got to her feet again, as gracefully as a woman seven months pregnant could..

Pacing, she again rubbed her belly.

“I’m all ears.” Regina watched her, looking at her as a patient and not a dear friend. She’d gained weight, maybe a little more than she should. Her ankles weren’t swollen and her skin looked fresh and dewy, where it wasn’t splotchy from crying.

“I don’t know where to begin.”

“Just start. When I have questions, we’ll cover it then.”

“I was afraid I’d lose Jimmy.” Regina moved to the edge of the couch, tucking her feet under her and clasping her hands between her knees. She suddenly had a frisson of fear, but curbed her impatience. She had to be wrong.

“I didn’t want to live without him or worry that he’d be taken from me.” Tracy stopped pacing and turned to face Reggie. “I started taking the serum after everything went to hell.”

To her credit, Reggie didn’t blink, she couldn’t. Nor could she breathe. Goddess, damned. This was another chapter they didn’t need written in the medical books. They hadn’t found much of interest in the hours of notes collected on the military experiment, and nothing had involved a female, except Regina, who’d been taking it without her knowledge or consent. To have Tracy admit to entering into the trial on purpose?

“So what has been happening?”

“I’m not sure.”

Regina got to her feet. “Grab a coat, we need a full workup and I want to see baby James.” She followed her own orders and turned to wait on Tracy as she slipped her feet into boots.

“You’re not yelling at me.” Tracy slung the handle of her purse over her shoulder.

“Should I be?” Regina checked the lock and closed the door behind them. Flurries danced in the slight breeze, leftovers from the major storm. She helped Tracy into her car, and then she moved behind the wheel. “I have to admit it’s a little late.”

“I know.” Tracy ran her hand through her hair, mussing the untamed fuzzy mass even more,

“What were you thinking?” Regina moved quickly through the traffic, heading for her office. She’d applied for a license and opened a private practice. Appointments only and open three days a week. The other two days she worked on continuing to learn about the experiment and what happened to the men who’d participated in it and lived.

“When did you start?”

“When the dust settled, after we lost Mitch. I started a diary.” Reaching into her purse, she pulled out a spiral notebook. The cover was tattered.

“How long did you take them?”

Silence filled the car until Regina wanted to shout.

She gripped the steering wheel and turned into the drive to her office. She pulled in and parked, finally turning to look at Tracy.

“Until yesterday morning.”

“Gods’ balls.” Regina got out of the car on the curse. Not waiting for Tracy, she turned off the alarm and locked the car as Tracy joined her on the covered porch.

Find more stories by Carol Shaughnessy in these anthologies:

Of Mountains and Mysteries
https://www.amazon.com/dp/B01GMGF9B0

The Cowboys of Clark's Folly
https://www.amazon.com/dp/B06XSCV32L

Rise of the Phoenix
https://www.amazon.com/dp/B074MPVSH6

About Carol Shaughnessy

Carol is a lifelong writer. Born in Vermont, she drifted south with her Navy husband until there was no snow to shovel. Now living in Georgia, she is lucky enough to be a full time writer. She heads a local writer's support group and was nominated for a Menage Award. She writes paranormal fiction, because vampires, werewolves, and dragons are hot!

When not traveling, cruising or flying to far off countries, Carol hosts weekend fires around a large pit. There friends and family gather, now and old, for wine, laugh, and s'mores.

Connect with Carol here:
www.amazon.com/Carol-Shaughnessy/e/B001r42BPI

Https://wwwifacebook.com/carol.shaughnessy.9

https://www.facebook.com/Sanctuary-19437079734913

Instagram:
@carolsexytales

Twitter
@carol_shaughnessy

92652010R00121

Made in the USA
Columbia, SC
02 April 2018